THE GRAVEDIGGERS' BREAD

PUSHKIN VERTIGO

FRÉDÉRIC DARD

TRANSLATED BY MELANIE FLORENCE

Pushkin Press
71–75 Shelton Street
London WC2H 9JQ

Original text © 1956 Fleuve Éditions,
département d'Univers Poche, Paris

English translation © Melanie Florence 2018

The Gravediggers' Bread was first published as
Le Pain des fossoyeurs in Paris in 1956

First published by Pushkin Press in 2018

1 3 5 7 9 8 6 4 2

ISBN 13: 978-1-78227-201-4

Designed and typeset by Tetragon, London
Printed and bound by CPI Group (UK) Ltd, Croydon CRO 4YY

www.pushkinpress.com

To François RICHARD
to thank him for the corrections
he has given me.

F.D.

PART ONE

1

You have to have waited patiently outside a telephone booth occupied by a woman to really appreciate just how much the fairer sex likes to talk.

I'd already been waiting my turn for a good ten minutes in that provincial post office that smelt of sadness, with only the sympathetic face of the switchboard girl to sustain me, when the lady in the booth finally ended the chatter she was paying for.

As it was a booth with frosted glass, until that point I'd had only her voice to go on in forming an impression of her.

I don't know why, but I had expected to see someone short, plump and awkward emerge. When she appeared, however, I realized how arrogant it is to think you can put together a picture of a person from their voice.

In reality, the person for whom I stood aside was a woman of around thirty, slim, blonde, with blue eyes that were slightly too large.

If she had lived in Paris she would have possessed the thing she most lacked, namely a certain sense of elegance. The white blouse she wore, and especially her black suit, the work of some elderly dressmaker with a subscription to the *Écho de la mode*, deprived her figure of eight-tenths of its power. You had to really love women, the way I did, to see that under her badly tailored garments this one had a waist like a napkin ring and admirable curves…

I was watching her walk away when the operator on the line gave a triumphant cry: "You're through to Paris!"

Being "through to Paris" in this case meant hearing the faint voice of my friend Fargeot peppered with intolerable crackling.

Because of the long-distance call he already knew it was me.

"Hello Blaise! I've been waiting for you to call... Well?"

I didn't answer straight away. In the booth there lingered a curious scent which moved me in a strange way. I breathed it in, half-closing my eyes... It conjured up many indefinable and fragile things... Vague things, things long gone which would never exist again and which almost made me feel like crying.

Fargeot's voice sizzled like a doughnut in boiling oil.

"Well then, out with it! Hello? I'm asking you..."

"No luck, my friend. The job was already gone."

His pained silence was renewed proof of the concern he had for me. He was a good guy. He had pointed out the job advertisement, then even lent me the fare.

"What do you expect?" I said consolingly. "I'm always last in the queue when they're giving things out."

He gave me an earful.

"You'll never get anywhere with an attitude like that, Blaise! You've got a loser's mentality. You delight in renunciation... The more life kicks you in the backside, the happier you are. A masochist, that's what you are."

I waited for the hothead to finish pouring out his resentment.

"Do you really think this is the moment for psycho-analysis, old pal?"

That shut him up. In a different tone, he asked, "When will you be back?"

"As soon as possible. It's as quiet as a rainy All Saints' Day in this godforsaken place."

"Have you got something to eat at least?"

"Don't you worry, my stomach has hidden resources."

"Fine, I'll expect you for dinner this evening. Don't lose heart, Blaise… Are you familiar with Azaïs's law?"

"Yes, life is split fifty-fifty between troubles and joys… Assuming that's right—and since I'm thirty now—that would at least suggest I'm sure to live to sixty!"

With that I hung up because the bell signalling the end of my three minutes was sounding in the earpiece.

Turning round to leave the booth, I felt something odd under my feet. It was a small crocodile-skin wallet. I picked it up, thinking to myself it was sure to contain anything but money. Before now chance had thrown purses in my path at moments when I was damned glad to find them; so far, though, they had contained nothing but devotional medals, trouser buttons or worthless foreign stamps.

Nevertheless, I slipped it into my pocket and went to pay the telephonist for my call, all the while pondering the possible contents of my find.

I made a swift exit from the post office… The station wasn't very far away. I had nowhere else to go, so I made my way there quickly. I was putting off going through the wallet just for the hell of it, so that I could enjoy a few delicious moments of hope. But once at the station, instead of getting my ticket home I hurried towards the toilets.

Feverishly opening the wallet, the first thing I discovered was a bundle of eight 1,000-franc notes folded in four.

"Blaise, my boy," I thought. "You've won the consolation prize."

I continued my investigations. From the other compartments I dug out an identity card in the name of Germaine Castain. It had the blonde woman's photo glued to it. In it she was younger and less pretty than a few moments ago... I looked at the picture, suddenly captivated by the woman's sad expression.

In addition, I found a tiny photo in the note section. It showed a man of my age, with heavy features. That was all the wallet contained. I was on the verge of throwing it into the lavatory bowl, having withdrawn the providential money first of course, when I remembered the woman's large, melancholy eyes...

I haven't always been very honest in my life and scruples have never kept me awake when I've been tired; however, I believe I've always been a gentleman when it comes to ladies.

I came out again with the wallet. An employee was glumly sweeping the tiled floor.

I went up to him. "Excuse me, do you know a lady called Germaine Castain?"

"Rue Haute?"

The card did indeed have this address on it. I gave him a cursory nod.

The employee waited for me to go on, leaning on his broom. He had a worn, infinitely bored expression.

"Does… er… does she live on her own?" I asked after a moment's hesitation.

The second question seemed to surprise him.

"Of course not," he said, sounding almost reproachful. "She's married to the undertakers."

It was my turn to be astounded.

"To the what?"

"To the underta—that is, to Castain, the director. You must know Castain? He's a right bad lot, another one."

The tone in which he'd said "another one" implied a great deal. I could see that for this poor drudge the world was made up of "bad lots".

"How do I get to Rue Haute?"

"Go across Place de la Gare… turn right into Rue Principale… straight on until it begins to go uphill. From that point on it's called Rue Haute."

I gave him a friendly little gesture of thanks and left, with the man's doubtful look fixed on my back.

When I'd been told at the rubber factory that the job I was going for had already been filled, my initial reaction had been one of intense relief. Provincial life does nothing for me; quite the reverse, it drags me down. Striding along the narrow streets of the town, I'd had the feeling I was plunging into a tunnel, and the idea of living here had filled me with terror. Only afterwards, on realizing that I had no job and no future, had I truly regretted arriving too late.

I chewed on my bitterness as I strolled across to Rue Haute. So what force for good was driving me to go and give back the wallet? To me the 8,000 francs were a godsend, whereas they wouldn't make a dent in the budget of that ill-turned-out little middle-class housewife. However much I thought about it, I couldn't understand my attitude.

Chance was kind enough to give me the wherewithal to get by for a few more days and I was declining the windfall? Was it from a need to shock the woman in the nasty black suit? Or...

With hindsight, I think my crisis of conscience owed more to the town than to Germaine Castain. I needed to create a happy memory to combat the disillusion aroused in me by this smug little place.

After a moment I noticed that Rue Principale was beginning to slope steeply upwards and an enamel plaque told me it was already Rue Haute.

Midday was striking just about everywhere in different tones. There was a lot of activity in the town's main thorough-fare. It was awakening a little from its accustomed lethargy. On the opposite pavement I spotted a mean little black shop whose door was decorated, if that's the right word, with a wreath painted in moss-green. White letters announced "Funeral Director".

I stopped, undecided: I could still turn round and go and catch my train in peace.

Then I noticed a small, dirty, sallow man lurking behind the windowpane, eyeing the passers-by as if they were the potential dead, which of course they were.

"The husband," I said to myself.

He looked like an old, sick rat. Life couldn't be much fun for the blonde with a companion like him.

The man gave off a whiff of nastiness. That was what decided me, I think. The possibility of pushing the door handle, the chance to get inside the lair and see a pretty woman with an air of resignation about her was easily worth 8,000 francs.

As I crossed the road I remembered the photograph inside the wallet and thought to myself that the blonde woman didn't necessarily want her husband to find it there, so I took it out of the compartment and slipped it into my pocket. Then I went up to the door and drove the yellowish little man back into the interior of his shop. The inside was even more wretched than the outside. It was cramped, dim, lugubrious and it smelt of death. There were death notices on the walls, along with coffin handles, crucifixes in metal or pearls, marble plaques with coats of arms, and artificial flowers, which together made the place look rather like a fairground shooting gallery. I stopped, looking at the small, yellowish man. He had grey hair, lying flat, a pointed nose with a red tip, and keen eyes. His thin lips twisted into what he hoped was a welcoming smile.

"Monsieur?"

"May I speak to Madame Germaine Castain?"

That took the wind out of his sails. Clearly no one had ever come asking for his wife. I thought he was going to ask me for an explanation, but he thought better of it and went over to the small door at the back.

When he opened it a smell of fried meat came out, tickling my taste buds.

"Germaine! Have you got a moment?"

From his voice I sensed he was not tender towards his wife. With pounding heart—God knows why—I stared at the door.

She had changed her black suit for a printed skirt which suited her a great deal better. Over it she had tied a little blue apron not much bigger than a pocket handkerchief. I found her a hundred times prettier done up like this.

"Monsieur would like to speak to you," Castain rasped.

She flushed, and looked at me fearfully. I guessed from her expression that my appearance seemed vaguely familiar but that she couldn't place me.

"I found a wallet which belongs to you," I murmured, pulling it out of my pocket.

She turned slightly pale.

"My God," she breathed. "So I'd lost it."

Naturally the coffin salesman lost his temper.

"You'll never change, will you, poor Germaine…"

He grew talkative.

"How can we ever thank you, monsieur? Is there money inside?"

"Yes."

He snatched the wallet out of his wife's hands. Her pallor intensified. It was a damn good thing, I thought, that I'd removed the photo of the guy with the thick-set features. For the moment it was a lot better off in my pocket than in Madame Castain's wallet. Sure enough, the undertaker thoroughly examined the crocodile-skin case.

16

"Eight thousand francs," he sighed. "Well, you're an honest man, monsieur, that's for sure."

The heartfelt thanks made me laugh.

"Aren't you going to thank monsieur, then?" exclaimed Castain.

"Thank you," she stammered.

She looked as if she was about to faint.

"There's really no need, anyone would have…"

"Where did you find it?" asked the husband.

His voice was filled with suspicion. The woman threw me a desperate glance.

"OK, sweetie," I thought. "You don't want me to mention the telephone booth."

Immediately I had made the connection between the little photo and the telephone call.

"I can't tell you," I replied. "I don't know the town."

I finished with a vague gesture. "Over that way, in the street."

I will never forget the look of wild gratitude she shot me. I had just made her life worth living again. Castain insisted on offering me an aperitif. I didn't object. It had been quite a while since I'd had a sniff of alcohol and I was in dire need of a drink.

We left the shop, went along a narrow corridor dimly lit by one feeble bulb, and emerged at last into a dining room so sad it made you want to scream.

"Please, do sit down."

I would have preferred to get the hell out of there. This dining room was like a tomb. It was long and narrow and its

17

only daylight came from a sort of hatch in the wall, opening onto a courtyard. The furniture was neither better nor worse than that usually found in the homes of small provincial shopkeepers, but within these walls with their yellowing wallpaper, the colour of incurable diseases, each piece as good as conjured up some funerary ornament. How the devil could a woman live in such a place?

Castain sat me down and poured me a glass of a bilious liquid he ingeniously dubbed "house aperitif". It was bitter and sugary at the same time and I had never swallowed a medicine as ghastly.

I was secretly cursing myself for my honesty while the graveyard rat was congratulating me on it. Deep down the situation was not without its piquancy.

"You're not from round here, then?" the yellowish man asked.

"No... Paris."

"Are you a sales representative?"

"I'd like to be... That's actually the reason I came to your town. A friend told me that the rubber factory was looking for a salesman. I've already worked in the chemical industry."

There was a dark disapproval in his voice when he asked, "In short, you're out of work?"

"In short, yes. Two years ago I left my job in Paris to work with a scoundrel who claimed to be setting up a building firm in Morocco. The few assets I had went into that. For two years I kicked my heels in a little office in Casablanca. It was unbearably hot and I never saw a soul, not even my associate… I came back last month. I had tried to find a job over there but with what's going on now the Frenchman is a commodity it's increasingly hard to find a place for… To cut a long story short, here I am back in France, out of money and out of work. It's no joke."

"Are you married?"

"No, fortunately."

I had spoken without thinking. I quickly turned to look at the young woman standing motionless against the door frame.

"I mean 'fortunately' for the woman who might have married me," I clarified.

She smiled at me. It was the first time, and to me it was as if a ray of light had come over the room.

"No success here then, with the job?" asked the undertaker.

"They'd just taken on a candidate who was quicker than me."

"Would you have liked to work in this area?"

"I'd like to work anywhere, especially here. I like this area. I just love the provinces."

That was all nonsense, obviously. I was only saying it to please them.

He took hold of his disgusting bottle of "house aperitif".

"Another little teardrop?"

He certainly spoke like a funeral director.

"No, really, I never usually drink."

He expressed his clear approval by lowering his eyelids briefly.

"You are so right… I understand. In my house, my father was an alcoholic and it was Achille Castain who paid the price."

And he added with a certain pride which, nevertheless, failed to impress, "Achille, that's me."

The moment had come to take my leave. The woman had scuttled back to her stove.

"Well, Monsieur Castain, it's been delightful to meet you."

"Thank you again."

We shook hands before we reached the shop doorway. His was dry and cold.

He didn't let go. His fingers were like the talons of a bird of prey.

"I wonder, monsieur…"

I realized then that I hadn't introduced myself.

"Blaise Delange."

I waited for him to continue, but he seemed to hesitate. There was something uncertain in his small, quick eyes, which must have been unusual for them.

"Did you want to say something?"

He was looking me up and down with great care, completely unabashed. I refrained from telling him where to get off.

"I may have a proposition for you."

"For me?"

"Yes, does that surprise you?"

"God… that depends on what it entails."

The blonde woman had come back from the kitchen, having poured a little water over her roast veal.

"Are you going?" she asked.

Her voice contained a vague regret. Her large eyes appeared even more sorrowful.

"I've got a train to catch."

But her husband interrupted. "Do you know what I was thinking, Germaine?"

He was addressing me, in fact, but talking to his wife simplified matters.

He cleared his throat and, without looking directly at me, went on: "I need someone to assist me because my health isn't all it could be. Since monsieur is looking for a job… it seems… until something in your line comes up…"

I swear I wanted to laugh. That was really the most extraordinary suggestion anyone had ever made to me! An undertaker, me? I saw myself with a cocked hat and buckle shoes, black cape over my shoulder, walking in front of a funeral procession. No, it was too ridiculous.

I stopped myself from laughing, however.

"Assist you in what?" I asked. "I don't know anything about your profession, Monsieur Castain, except that it's not exactly a bundle of laughs."

"You're making a mistake there, it's as good as any other."

I'd offended him. Like everyone with stomach problems, he was over-sensitive.

"I'm not denying that, but I still believe yours demands certain, er, talents that I in no way possess."

"But which you can acquire. Of course there's no question of you organizing funerals, but our trade includes a certain sales side which tires me out. Our work, you see, begins with a catalogue. We sell tangible things, Monsieur Delange. Are you afraid of the dead?"

In a flash I went through the list of all the dead people I knew.

"I wouldn't say afraid… I… they intimidate me."

"That timidity is easily got rid of, believe me. I was like you to begin with. And then you get used to it."

He shrugged his shoulders.

"I'm well aware that the layman imagines all sorts of things about our profession. Or rather, he finds it hard to admit it's an ordinary profession. Yet I can assure you that gravediggers' bread tastes just the same as other people's."

At that moment the telephone rang in the shop and he went to answer it.

I found myself alone with his wife. I took out the photograph, which was still in my pocket, and handed it to her discreetly.

"Here, before I go…"

She hastily slipped it into the neck of her blouse.

"Thank you," she stammered.

For some time we stood looking at each other without a word. She was the kind of woman you long to see slightly unhappy so that you can console her. The click signalling the end of the phone call sounded.

"Stay," she breathed.

Did she really say that? I'm not sure. Even now I wonder whether I guessed at rather than heard the word. It set my blood on fire.

Castain returned, with a satisfied air.

"That was a call about a client," he crowed. "The good thing about our profession is that we're protected against unemployment, you see. Of course, we had a little dip when penicillin came along and these new sulphonamides aren't doing us much good, but other than that… What do you say?"

I sensed the woman's intense eyes on me. I didn't dare look at her.

"We can always give it a try," I sighed.

2

He wasn't offering me a king's ransom, of course: 20,000 francs per month, plus lunch and a ridiculous percentage on business I brought in above a certain value.

Castain assured me that I could, in this way, increase my monthly salary by some 1,200 francs. Taking into account the much-vaunted midday meal, that would add up to a decent sum in total.

The undertaker assured me that in this backwater I could live like a prince on such an income. He knew a small hotel where I could find lodgings at a good price. In short, the more reluctant he saw me to be, the more enthusiastically he praised this new existence.

"And, after all," he finished, "if things don't work out we can still always go our separate ways, can't we?"

I agreed.

"Right. So you'll go to Paris and come straight back with your trunk?"

I'd thought to myself that if I set foot in the capital again I'd never be able to tear myself away to come and bury myself—or, rather, bury other people—here in the back of beyond.

"It's not worth it. I've a friend who can send my things on. If you'll permit me, I can phone him."

"Call him right away."

Castain was delighted. His wife set another place while I was waiting to be connected. The delicious meat smell got

24

my juices going. I hadn't eaten very much for some time and a proper meal was rather tempting.

I got through to Fargeot and explained very briefly that I had found a job to tide me over.

"In what line?" He sounded worried.

"At the funeral director's!"

"No, be serious."

"I'm deadly serious… I'm going to sell coffins, my old pal. You'd never imagine what nice ones you can get."

As I spoke, I was looking at the samples pinned to the walls of the sinister shop.

"So much so," I went on, "that it breaks your heart to stick them in the ground."

We agreed arrangements to settle the bill for my boarding house in Boulevard de Port-Royal and he said he'd see about sending on my suitcase that same day.

With my mind at rest over this, I joined my hosts at table.

It was a convivial meal. Castain was overexcited by my presence.

"By the way, do you drive?"

"Yes, why?"

"I'm thinking of the hearse. I have someone for the funerals, of course, but he works as and when. Aside from those, there are private transfers, if you get my drift. Changes of tomb, deliveries to the morgue…"

Germaine Castain was giving me glances of silent encouragement. She sensed how barbaric such language appeared to me and was doing her best to sweeten it. I think she understood that I had accepted because of her. That made things easier between us in one way. But it made them a hell of a lot more complicated in another!

I was impatient to find myself alone with her for a decent length of time so that I could ask her about her life. This strange couple concealed a mystery, and I was eager to find it out.

But the hoped-for tête-à-tête didn't happen that day. In the afternoon Castain took me first to the Hôtel de la Gare where, on the strength of their friendship, he persuaded the manager to give me a room overlooking the street for the price of one on the railway line.

Next we went to see the clients who had phoned that morning. These were well-to-do people, the owners of a sawmill, if I remember correctly. The grandfather had died in the early hours. Before crossing the threshold of their house, my boss gave me a lesson in applied psychology.

"You see, Delange," he said. "We can't expect anything on the business front here. It will be the second-lowest category and a pauper's coffin."

"Why do you foresee that?"

"The fact that it's the grandfather. That's ten years now they've been spoon-feeding him and changing his sheets three times a day. If they could they'd stick him in the dustbin. You'll see."

He rapped on the door with the old brass knocker and a wrinkled maid came to open the door, weeping for form's sake. She led us to the room where the family were receiving neighbours to view the deceased and recounting his death for the twentieth time.

The dead man's son, a tall, red-faced fellow with hair that was already white, took us into the dining room. Without asking, he set three glasses on the table and reached for an old bottle of Burgundy which had been brought out of the cellar to await us. While the master of the house was busy looking for a corkscrew, Castain whispered in my ear: "It's these bastards that are killing me with their obsession with offering drinks. And you can't refuse or they get annoyed."

"Let us move on to the cruel necessities of the occasion," he intoned, words he clearly had off pat.

The feigned sorrow on his face made me giggle. He noticed and shot me a furious glance. From his briefcase he was extracting a small portfolio containing photographs of caskets, catafalques, crucifixes and other funerary accoutrements.

"What do you have in mind, Monsieur Richard?"

The big red-faced man shook his head.

"Just what's strictly necessary," he declared straight out. "You knew my father? He had simple tastes."

Another knowing look from Castain. In his eyes was written in block capitals: I TOLD YOU SO.

He nonetheless sighed: "Do you think so?"

When it came to talking business he was a real idiot, I thought. That got me angry.

"Monsieur Richard," I started. "The strictly necessary is something you can do yourself. You have planks—all you need to do is put four of them together and you've got it.

What we, on the other hand, provide is a way of paying one last tribute to your father, and of proving to your nearest and dearest that you considered him more than just a burdensome old man!"

Castain was aghast. His mean little eyes grew huge and I saw myself distorted in them as in some diabolical mirror. His right shoe was desperately searching for my left, which I'd carefully tucked up onto a bar of my chair. As for our customer, after jerking upright in his seat, he suddenly appeared very downcast.

"To be sure," he murmured. "To be sure, I'm not saying…"

I'd got into my stride, and to be honest I could sense the fellow was in my thrall. Plus, for my own part I was keen to savour the humour of this unusual profession.

"But Monsieur Richard, you *are* saying… and you're saying, 'what's strictly necessary'. I won't do you the insult of believing that you're motivated by saving money in circumstances like these, and you won't do me that of thinking that I want to take advantage of your grief. But let's face up to things. You have just lost the one to whom you owe everything. What would people think if they saw you giving him a hasty burial, hmm? You know them. Always ready to gossip and put people down. They'd say you were ungrateful or—and this would be worse for your standing—they'd say you lack the means to put on a good show."

That was a direct hit, not to his heart but to his pride.

"You're right," he declared.

And, to Castain, "He's right. And I like people who speak their mind. Does he work for you?"

"Yes," said Castain, astonished to see how easily I'd triumphed. "He's from Paris."

After that he had only to take out his order book and announce the prices. The man who sold planks was ripe for the picking. I think if we'd had a parade of the Republican Guard in our catalogue we'd have sold him them along with the rest.

When we left, Castain said nothing for some time. Irritated by his silence, I provoked him:

"Well boss, how was that for starters?"

He stopped walking. With a shrug of the shoulders he murmured:

"Your methods are a little brutal... But in any case, the results are terrific!"

"Isn't that all that matters?"

"Indeed. But some people in Richard's place wouldn't have stood for it."

"So? What does that matter, since you don't have any competition? No, Monsieur Castain, the clientele likes to be chivvied. Most people are bad at making decisions so they're grateful if you do it for them."

He wasn't entirely convinced.

He retreated into sullen silence until we got back. Germaine was minding the shop. She was doing accounts at an ink-stained writing desk. When she saw me her eyes lit up with happiness.

"He's a winner!" declared Castain, hooking his felt hat with its upturned brim onto a coffin handle. "You know big Richard from the sawmill? He's a tough guy, eh? Well, he'd won him over in no time."

I hadn't anticipated such an outburst of enthusiasm.

"Will you stay for dinner?" suggested the sallow little man.

I avoided looking at the woman.

"No, let's stick to what we agreed, lunches only. In any case, I'm very tired and thinking of an early night."

He didn't insist.

"As you wish… Would you like an advance on your salary?"

"Not for the moment. We'll discuss it later."

"All right."

I took my leave with a vague feeling of guilt towards the woman. In leaving her I felt I was abandoning her deep in a lonely cemetery or in some chamber of horrors where her discreet charm would simply fade away.

The dining room at the Hôtel de la Gare was very conventional, but had a certain good-humoured intimacy about it. This atmosphere made a happy contrast with Castain's shop. I ate the set menu at a communal table along with some travelling salesmen and a temporary schoolmaster.

After peeling an over-ripe pear, pretentiously called "dessert" on the menu, I felt a need to enjoy my own company in a shadowy corner.

In addition to which, it was still too early for bed. I decided to go to the station to buy something to help me get to sleep, namely cigarettes and magazines.

It was a beautiful spring night, vast and blue, with unknown stars and scents wafting by on the ripples of the breeze. From the hotel doorway I began to breathe the night in almost voluptuously. It reassured me.

I was inhaling for the third time, when I noticed a voice calling me in the darkness.

"Monsieur Blaise!"

I turned to my right. There was a hedge of privet bushes in boxes bordering a terrace. I made out a shape and the light patch of a face. Again the voice called, "Monsieur Blaise."

I moved forwards then into the shadows and recognized Germaine Castain.

She was standing motionless against the wall of the hotel, beneath the dining-room window. An old coat was thrown round her shoulders, and her hair—perhaps because of the breeze—was in a mess. Her eyes had a strange shine to them. On closer inspection I could see she'd been crying.

"Madame Castain," I murmured. "What's the matter?"

Instead of replying she made for the area set back from the square. Here the station concourse formed a cul-de-sac because of the railway track. There was the embankment, the plane trees, the cubic form of a transformer box.

We stopped behind the transformer. All of a sudden my heart was racing. I longed to take her in my arms.

"Why are you crying?"

"I'm not crying."

"Yes you are."

She used her fingertips to check.

"Forgive me for calling you Blaise—I don't remember your surname."

"Not at all, I'm glad you did. Answer me, why were you crying?"

31

"Because he's hit me again!"

I couldn't believe my ears.

"He beats you?"

"Yes, often."

I was alarmed. Certainly I'd suspected that life with Castain must be lacking in charm for his wife, but I had never dreamt he was knocking her about!

I clenched my fists.

"That horrible man. Daring to lay hands on you—why does he hit you?"

Her face was serious now. She had regained her self-control and looked thoughtful.

"Because," she said finally, "because it brings him a bit of relief, I think. The weak take revenge for their weakness on those who are even weaker."

I asked her the question which was eating me up, and truthfully I didn't believe I could put it so crudely: "Why the devil did you go and marry that fellow? You're like chalk and cheese!"

A train passed slowly by at the top of the embankment in a paroxysm of asthmatic puffing. Its red glow set Germaine's face on fire and I saw that her eyes had an angry glint in them.

"Why does a young girl marry a dried-up old man? Just read one of the stories you see in the magazines. I was young… I loved a boy my own age… he got me pregnant. His family were against our marriage and sent him abroad somewhere so he'd forget me. Ever since I was a little girl Castain had been cornering me in dark places. He took advantage of the situation to ask my mother for my hand in marriage. The dear woman was a poor widow, in despair over the mistake I'd made. She was so insistent I jump at this generous offer that I accepted. Only, you have to beware of devout people. They're the worst bastards on earth."

From her lips the word "bastard" took on a wider meaning. It summed up all her rancour, all her immense despair.

I put my hand on her shoulder. She shook me off.

To hide my embarrassment, I asked: "And then?"

"Then, nothing. His age, his position and his feigned generous heart meant that every right was on his side. He began by taking me to see some midwife who specialized in 'premature births'. I didn't have the child. Castain won right across the board. He's always treated me like a dog. Now whenever he feels like it he seizes on the first opportunity that comes along to beat me."

This story lacked poetry. It was like a drama from a Zola novel that shocks both intelligent people and the vulgar bourgeois.

We remained motionless for some time, without a word. Another train went past and each of its carriage windows lit up Madame Castain's beautiful, sad face.

"Why haven't you left him?"

She tossed her blonde hair. I felt a lock brush my face and once again I resisted the desire to hold her close, cradling her pain.

"You see, Monsieur Blaise…"

"You can just call me Blaise."

"That wouldn't be proper."

"OK, no need to say another word about it, it's all becoming clear. You stayed because one scandal was enough to fill your little life of inactivity, isn't that so?"

I had spoken harshly. She moved away from me.

"Why are you being unkind?"

"I'm not being unkind, I'm indignant. I like the people I associate with to have some sense of dignity. I think it's disgusting that you let yourself be beaten like… well like a dog, actually!"

I thought she would run off, but she didn't even flinch. I went on: "Besides, a little bird tells me you've got some compensations, isn't that right?"

"What do you mean by that?"

"I'm thinking of the photo hidden in your wallet. I'm also thinking of your phone call at the post office, because that's where I saw you."

"Yes, I know."

"If I hadn't used my head I could have given your undertaker good reason to give you a beating you wouldn't forget in a hurry, couldn't I?"

"That's true… yes. You're very clever, Blaise, and very sensitive. Your thoughtfulness…"

"Never mind my thoughtfulness! Answer me: you have a lover, haven't you? A woman who goes to the post office to make calls when she has a telephone at home doesn't want to be overheard by her husband."

Her voice sounded strict: "I *do* have a lover, yes."

"I'm not reproaching you. I'd even say I approve entirely…"

"Thanks!" she said ironically.

"Who's the lucky man?"

You may or may not believe me, but jealousy was gnawing at my insides. Yes, I was jealous over this girl I hadn't even laid eyes on twelve hours before.

"Still the same one," she replied.

I didn't understand immediately.

"Huh?"

"Still the same one… the father of the baby I didn't have."

My anger leapt to life again, full, vehement.

"When I mentioned your lack of dignity I didn't think it was *that* complete. So here's a pathetic guy who drops you after he's got you pregnant. He allows you to marry that rotten, dried-up fool Castain, to waste away surrounded by your funeral wreaths, and the swine continues to have his fill of you!"

"Be quiet!"

In a whisper she murmured, "You wouldn't understand."

"Please God there's something *to* understand!"

"He's ill. He has been all his life… epileptic fits."

I said nothing. The problem might have a new complexion to it but in my eyes it remained insoluble.

"So you're the mistress of an epileptic?"

"So? He's a man like any other, isn't he?"

Her cry was so heart-rending that it moved me. I shook my head.

"All right, he's a man like any other man. A man with a right to happiness. A man with extenuating circumstances. But humanity isn't pretty, Germaine. You'll never prevent a

35

normal man from thinking it's a shame to see a beautiful girl give herself to a sick man."

I was thinking now that old Castain hadn't been so wrong to get rid of the child after all; deep inside myself I was making excuses for him.

She was speaking. I made an effort to listen to what she was saying.

"He was handsome. I'd always loved him. People told me he had epileptic fits but I didn't care. Even when I witnessed one of his fits I wasn't scared. It was just that at the time of our affair his family used his illness as an excuse to send him away. He had an attack, they injected him with a sedative which destroyed all his willpower. They told him I'd married a very rich old skinflint—Castain *is* rich. Maurice extended his stay in Switzerland. Years passed. Then his father died and he came back. A few months ago I saw him again. We were irresistibly driven into each other's arms. It all started again."

She fell silent. I felt ill at learning all that and decided that the very next day I would clear off back to Paris. I didn't think I could live somewhere like this.

"Hang on, since your Casanova's come back, can't you disappear off somewhere with him?"

"No."

"Why?"

"Because he's ruined. His father was riddled with debts when he died. Maurice lives in a garret. He makes a living through photography but it's a poor living. I… I help him."

This just got better! Madame had her fingers in the funeral director's till in order to put food on the cheap pimp's table!

I was sickened. All three of them, Maurice, Germaine and the dreaded Achille seemed like a bunch of spineless cowards and degenerates. Yes, there was a definite lack of oxygen round here.

Something struck me: "Why are you telling me all this?"

"Well, I…"

"Come on, spit it out."

"Just now, when he'd hit me, I told him I'd had enough of his behaviour. I ran away to… to give him a fright. That's the first time I've acted like this. I hope it'll make him calm down. But I'm going back."

"And why did you dare, today?"

"Because of you. Since you've been here I feel stronger. It seems to me, and besides you've proved it, that you're my friend."

"Yes, I am your friend."

"So I'm going to ask you to do something else for me."

"Fire away."

"It's difficult to say…"

"After what you've already confided in me, I can't imagine what could be difficult to express, sweetie."

"That's true. Here goes then. Tomorrow it's market day in Pont-de-l'Air."

"Where?"

"Pont-de-l'Air. A big town near here. On Thursdays I take the bus there to do the weekly shopping, because groceries are cheaper there than here. Maurice lives in Pont-de-l'Air."

"I get it. So Thursday's the day for your frolics."

My sardonic tone, more than the word itself, hit home.

She turned on her heel and strode off into the shadows. I was stupefied for a moment, then ran after her. I caught hold of her arm.

"Hey, wait, Germaine! No need to be that sensitive! When you claim a man's friendship you must expect some bluntness on his part. That's what distinguishes friendship from love. In love you only use thistledown, in friendship you use horsehair as well."

She stopped.

"Yes, you're right… Forgive me, my nerves are in shreds."

"Not as much as mine are!"

It had just slipped out. She looked at me.

"Why's that?"

"It may have escaped your notice but I have seriously fallen for you. I'm going to confide in you as well, open a window onto my personality. If I hadn't seen you at the post office, you could have kissed goodbye to your eight thousand francs."

She was shocked, of course.

"Oh, that's what you say…"

"I'm saying that because it's God's honest truth, that's all. A simple clarification in passing. Now, go on—what do you want from me?"

"The row with Achille just now came about because of the market. He announced that it was ridiculous for me to go to Pont-de-l'Air just to make a small saving. I think he must suspect something. I insisted, and he got angry. Tomorrow he'll prevent me from going, that's for sure."

"So you'd like me to go over there and explain things to Maurice?"

"You've guessed it. Is that a nuisance?"

"No, not exactly… But are you forgetting that I have a boss?"

"That doesn't matter. Tomorrow morning you come and tell him your trunk hasn't arrived and that you have to go and fetch it from Paris. Here, there's money in this envelope. Take your expenses from it and hand the rest over to him."

"Understood. Where does lover boy live?"

"His surname is Thuillier. His address is 3, Rue Marius-Lesœur in Pont-de-l'Air—will you remember?"

"Eternally. You can count on me."

"Good, I'm going home."

"Would you like me to walk with you?"

"Better not."

"As you wish."

She was hopping from one foot to the other, unable to make up her mind to go.

"Have you got something else to tell me?"

"No. Make sure to explain to him that… as soon as I can… and I'll try to phone him tomorrow."

I made a little gesture of agreement.

"What are you thinking?"

"I'm thinking he's a damned lucky man."

She held out her hand.

"Thank you. Good night!"

"Good night."

She slunk away under the trees with their sprinkling of fat buds. I felt a bit depressed once she'd disappeared.

The lights had just gone out in the hotel and there was only the night light in the hall. I reached my room without making a noise. It was small, pink, clean and smelt of trains.

I undressed completely and slid between the rough sheets. It was a long time before I fell asleep, however. Whenever a train went by, everything in the room shook even though my window didn't overlook the tracks.

I tried to imagine the drowsy people passing in a clanking of metal, but for me they were without souls and without faces.

3

The next day at the Castains' there was no trace of their bust-up the evening before. I arrived to find Germaine polishing the rococo furniture in the dining room and Achille preparing for the Richard grandfather's funeral.

I told him my friend had been unable to get into my room without a key and that the easiest thing was for me to make a return trip to Paris to fetch my cases. Castain didn't bat an eyelid, just told me to be quick because he was counting on me for the next day.

I was therefore able to take the bus to Pont-de-l'Air without difficulty.

The place was the replica of the one I had just left. There was the same Place de la Gare, with an Hôtel de la Gare; the same Rue Principale, the same old-fashioned shops and, above all, the same quiet people.

I asked the way to Rue Marius-Lesœur of a small boy, who led me there by the hand. This was a narrow street at a crossroads marked by a flashing light in the middle. It was lined with bulging old houses which were not without character. I set off across the cobbles in search of number 3.

I arrived at a sort of grand town house whose enormous door reminded me of a prison. I rang. A forbidding lady answered. When I told her that I wished to see Monsieur

Maurice Thuillier she replied haughtily that I would have to go through the stables and up some wooden stairs.

The young man's living quarters in fact clearly belonged to a different world from this austere residence. They had been built above abandoned stables now used to store cars. Evidently the owners of the town house were either stingy or of limited means; they exploited every possibility to create an income for themselves by letting the parts of the building which did not impinge on their grandeur.

The wooden staircase creaked under my weight. Its iron rail was wobbly and wouldn't have withstood the stumbling of a drunken man. The narrow steps led up to a worm-eaten balcony with several doors leading off it.

At the top of the stairs I called out: "Monsieur Thuillier, please!"

The first door was flung open and *he* appeared. He was a great deal more handsome than in his photo—a great deal more handsome than me as well! That realization struck me straight off.

Tall and athletic, he was wearing corduroy trousers, a red and white checked shirt and sports shoes.

He had dark, feverish eyes, light-coloured hair cut very short, and his mouth was flanked by two deep lines. Thuillier was standing in front of me like a dog ready to bite.

"Was it you calling me?"

"Yes."

"What do you want with me?"

"If you invited me in I'd be more comfortable telling you."

I thought he was about to throw me over the rickety banister. But he restrained himself.

"Oh, come in then… You know, it's not the Ritz."

"I couldn't care less."

That calmed him down. He smiled at me.

"I've never seen you…"

"Me neither. There's a first time for everything though, isn't there?"

"Who are you?"

"A colleague of Monsieur Achille Castain. D'you know him?"

He was on his guard. His upper lip drew back in a snarl and again he looked like a vicious dog.

The dwelling was in keeping with the man. It was furnished with a mattress laid on the floor and covered with a large cashmere blanket. There was also an ancient table, a very beautiful Louis XIV chest of drawers and a dressing table on which he had placed all the equipment for a photographic laboratory. The walls were almost entirely covered in prints, many of which proved interesting.

I had taken in the layout of the place at a glance. The lodging's only source of daylight was the glass door. It was dim and thus particularly suited, of course, to a photographer.

Standing square in front of me, hands on hips, Thuillier was looking at me through eyes streaked with red veins.

"Monsieur Achille Castain's colleague, otherwise known as the undertaker's assistant. And as well as manhandling the corpses, you dabble in espionage to fill your free time?"

I fought back my sudden desire to bring my fist into contact with his handsome face.

"Any espionage I do is on Madame Castain's behalf."

I took out the envelope she'd given me and threw it down on the table.

"Her husband stopped her from coming to be made love to today—would you be so kind as to excuse her?"

I saw the heartbreak in his eyes. He must have been wildly impatient for her to arrive. That was why he'd received me so brusquely.

He stuttered "Eh? What?"

"I told you, there was a row at home last night about Pont-de-l'Air. He doesn't want her to come—probably got wind of something. I was the only means she had of letting you know in time, have you got that?"

He squinted at the envelope.

"What's that?"

He knew—I could tell from his evasive look—but he wanted to find out if I knew the score.

I didn't like the guy. He may have been an invalid, but I was quite certain he was an idler of the first order. He wasn't worth a damn, as he'd amply proved. As a woman in love, Germaine dressed him up in all the fine qualities she wished for in a man; nonetheless he belonged to the ranks of those little good-for-nothings who take advantage of credulous women.

"That," I said flippantly, "is your week's fodder."

He came towards me. "What did you say?"

He thought he could intimidate me, but he could take a

jump! I was ready for him, old Maurice. At the first sign of physical aggression, I was resolved to go for him, head first!

"It's your fodder," I said. "Dead man's bread, you might call it. The tithe madame takes from Castain's corpses."

He snatched up the envelope, tore it open and pulled out 4,000 francs. A grimace of disappointment twisted that very mobile upper lip.

"Not much, is it? You'd do better to work a dowager on the Côte d'Azur… Germaine does what she can, but with her skinflint of a gravedigger it won't go far."

"Bugger off!" he snarled.

"With pleasure."

I turned to go. I already had one foot on the top step of the wooden staircase when he called me back:

"Hey!"

"Are you calling me or your dog?"

"Just listen for a moment."

I hesitated, then went back into the room. An unpleasant smell of hyposulphite hung in the air. I hadn't noticed it at first.

"What?"

"Have you been working for Castain for long? She's never mentioned you."

"Since yesterday."

He thought I was making fun of him.

"Since yesterday?"

"Yes. Are you shocked that Germaine has already confided her intimate secrets to me? I've a face which inspires trust in ladies—and *I* don't abuse it."

"Oh you can stop your jibes—they don't get to me."

"I'm sure—the thing about guys of your sort is that they're impervious."

"Have you said your piece? *I'm* not insulting *you*, am I?"

That was the best he could come up with.

"You don't insult your mistress's confidant."

He was white with suppressed anger.

"I don't give a damn what you think. You can go to hell!"

I took two steps forwards and gave his face a resounding slap. He put his hand up to his left cheek, which was turning red.

We had nothing more to say to each other after that. I took my leave. But just as I was about to go through the porch of the former stables, I heard a horrendous racket coming from his place. I stopped, undecided. The forbidding woman who had opened the front door to me appeared. She was listening.

"He's having one of his attacks," she sighed. "He has them more and more often. I tell him he should see a doctor but he sends me packing, saying I'm telling lies. He doesn't remember anything about it afterwards of course."

She went back in with a shrug. I leapt up the stairs and froze in the doorway. Frankly, it wasn't a pretty sight.

Maurice was writhing on the floor, thrashing about like a devil. His eyes were wild, staring, bulging out of their sockets. White froth was forming on his lips and he was bucking, scraping the floor without uttering a sound. This sort of struggle with nothingness had something terrible about it.

And yet I felt no pity for him.

"So that's the creature she loves," I mused. "My God, is it possible that such a woman's every thought is for this poor devil?"

I stepped over Maurice and made my way to the dressing table-cum-laboratory, a Machiavellian notion going through my mind. On the marble, in front of the baths of emulsion, was a Rolleiflex with an electronic flash. I looked to see what stage the reel of film was at. The number four came up in the little round hole when I'd pressed the focusing button.

I set the exposure and plugged the flash into its battery. And then I treated myself to three photographs of the guy at the height of his spasms.

If he called his landlady a liar when she spoke about his fits, this way he'd have firm proof of her sincerity.

I put the camera back on the dressing table. Things were quietening down for Maurice. The jerking was stopping and he was panting on the floor. A thread of foul spit dripped from his mouth. His nose was running, his face was smeared with dust and froth.

I nudged him a bit with the toe of my shoe.

"Well then, Don Juan, how are we?"

I felt as fierce as life. He gave me a completely vacant look. I made my way round him the way you make your way round a piece of rubbish that turns your stomach, and went out to breathe the mild provincial air. I damn well needed to, I can tell you!

4

If my alibi was to be credible, I couldn't very well return to the Castains' before the next day. So I strolled around Pont-de-l'Air until the evening, having lunch in a country bistro, sauntering along a canal, reading newspapers which had no interest for me. Germaine had entrusted me with a nasty job, and I felt slightly resentful towards her. The one thing that cheered me up was thinking of Thuillier's face when he developed his photos. When he saw himself he wouldn't believe his eyes. That would give the damn show-off a shock! My own cruelty surprised me, because by and large I'm quite a nice guy. Only I was smitten with Germaine and could not accept her weakness with Maurice.

That empty day seemed never-ending, so I was very glad to return to the fold. The Hôtel de la Gare felt almost like a safe haven to me. I no longer had any desire to leave my position; it had a seductive side to it.

The next morning, very early, I went to retrieve my cases from the station. They had arrived the previous day. Next I changed my clothes, as my underwear really wasn't too fresh. In a white shirt, dressed in a navy-blue suit and with a black tie—as befits a gentleman who makes a living from grief—I presented myself at the Castains'.

The shop wasn't yet open and I had to knock on the wooden shutter. Light-footed Achille came to let me in, wearing a grey brushed-cotton waistcoat and comfortable fur-lined slippers.

"You already!" he exclaimed.

"Yes, am I too early?"

"That's not a bad thing! You can have some coffee with me."

I went into the hideous little shop which smelt of dead people. We made our way through to the dining room, where Germaine was laying out bowls for breakfast. She had her hair tied up in a ribbon and was wearing a big red dressing gown.

I looked at her and a warm caress ran through my body. She looked at me too…

"Good trip?" Castain asked.

"Excellent, if a bit brief."

He gave an ugly little laugh.

"Do you know?"

"What?"

And he suddenly went quiet, then, almost simpering but seeming more embarrassed than anything:

"I'd got it into my head that you wouldn't come back."

I looked at him: "The very idea!"

"I had. I thought the work wasn't to your taste. Obviously it's off-putting at the start. But you'll see, you get used to it very quickly and very well. Like every trade, when you practise it diligently you begin to love it."

He was touching. I felt I meant something to him. I'd impressed him with my casual ways, my direct manner and my well-cut suits.

"Well, as you see, I'm here. Ready to get stuck in. Speaking of which, are there any new deaths in the neighbourhood?"

"Yes, a butcher's wife. We're going to try an experiment."

"What kind of experiment?"

"You'll go on your own to offer our services. Anyway, I'm busy with the Richard funeral this morning."

He turned to Germaine.

"And you, do me the pleasure of getting dressed, eh? I'll be leaving in ten minutes and I don't want to see you in the shop in your dressing gown!"

She nodded in agreement.

"Right, I'll dress first."

"Look, Delange, you'll wait until my wife is dressed before you leave. I've put the butcher's address on my desk ready for you—it's less than a hundred metres away."

He swallowed his bowl of coffee while I carefully buttered my *biscottes*. I was delighted by the thought of remaining alone with Germaine for a moment; that was unhoped for! She seemed content with the unforeseen blessing as well, but for different reasons. She was thinking I would be able to give her an account of my "mission" in detail. Although not a muscle in her face moved, I could see from the way her fingers were trembling that she was all keyed up.

I avoided looking at her during the time it took for Castain to get ready. When he came out of his room, dressed in a black uniform and a cocked hat, I just burst out laughing. He looked like a Walt Disney character: he was exactly like a gnome in disguise.

"Are you making fun of me?"

"No, but it's just so funny for me to see you in that get-up. Don't you feel—I don't know—comical?"

"Not at all!"

"What a masquerade these funerals are! They deprive death of all its gravitas. I think it's a sort of defence mechanism that has made people all round the world turn them into a grand spectacle. All this play-acting just to make themselves seem important."

My virulence terrified them both, and they looked anxiously at me.

"Well then, you're quite the anarchist," scolded Castain.

"I'm objective, that's all. And when a man's objective then he's necessarily humble about what his life's worth. You're not going to tell me that you believe in all this? All this pomp and show that aims for solemnity and dignity, but ends up looking ridiculous? Look at yourself in the mirror. Anyone would think you were off to a masked ball."

He shrugged his shoulders.

"Oh, these Parisians…"

I was quick to reassure him.

"In any case, don't be scared, I'm not going to let the clientele know my own personal view. What kind of man is this butcher, by the way?"

As soon as I became professional he relaxed.

"The wealthy kind!"

"So all the frills then?"

"Yes, if you can overcome his sense of thrift. I've left the prices out for you—mug up on them before you turn up over there."

With that he left.

He trusted me enough to leave me alone with his wife before she was dressed. Castain was a simple soul at heart. Once I had given him evidence of my honesty at the outset he generalized this virtue and believed me to be proof against all temptations.

When the shop door had closed, Germaine went to make sure he really was going away. Then she returned to the dining room. I was just finishing at table. I wiped my mouth and stood up.

"You're itching to know, eh?"

"I wasn't able to call him yesterday."

"Castain sometimes goes out, though."

"When he goes out, I mind the shop and can't get to the post office."

"But you have a phone here!"

"Yes, it's just that any non-local calls are listed and he goes through everything meticulously."

"Understood."

"So?"

Her impatience was irritating me.

"So nothing! I saw the bird. He wasn't happy… I was a big disappointment. He was expecting to make love and it's always saddening to find you've been dealt the wrong hand. He was also expecting more money. Four thousand francs seems more like a tip, don't you think?"

I thought she was going to show some embarrassment. Instead, she naively felt compelled to justify herself.

"That was all I could manage. Did you tell him that?"

This was too much.

"Tell me, Madame Castain, are you some kind of dimwit by any chance? I'm warning you now: I have a weakness for pretty women, but not when they're idiots!"

She went "Oh!", like a shocked Englishwoman.

I went up to her.

"You do realize that at your age you're behaving like a foolish old woman? Tradition dictates that women who keep a gigolo are elderly ladies of leisure. Or else they're whores. You, however, do not belong to either of those species."

She was too outraged to reply.

"I had a miserable day yesterday because of you! I thought about the role you were playing with that miserable wretch and that put me into one hell of a fury. Shall I tell you what I think? OK, that undertaker of yours is quite right to give you a good hiding. You're exactly the kind of girl that's made to be thrashed. Do you hear me?"

"Get out!" she screamed, pointing to the door.

She must have seen that in some B-movie. I shrugged.

"If I did go, you might be the loser! You need your little messenger boy, dear. Believe me, you won't have to send me away, because I'm starting to think I've had my fill of your mouldy little life."

I took hold of her arm and shook her.

"Do you understand me, you idiot? Enough! Oh and by the way, what a swell he is, madame's gigolo! I saw him having one of his little fits…"

"He had a fit?"

"Yes. The whole works. But don't worry, he recovered."

She turned pale. Her face looked somehow stupefied.

She finally looked up at me with those large blue eyes I found so moving.

"You hate him, don't you?"

I shrugged at that.

"Can you hate what you despise?"

"Are you a strong man?"

"I'm a man, simply and solely. Nothing but an ordinary little man. It's that Maurice who's nothing. And I'm insulting nothingness!"

"You despise him because he's ill!"

"Good God no, quite the reverse—that would make him of interest to me. Only I can't tolerate the arrogant and cowardly way he behaves. He takes himself for someone interesting and he waits to snaffle the three sous that you scrape together from poor Castain. He got you pregnant in the past and dropped you, only too pleased that Maman and Papa disapproved. Despite that, he's now happy to accept your love and your dough. Listen, Germaine, I don't want to hear another word about that bastard. I think if I went to see him again I'd smash his face in. Understood?"

"Have no fear, I won't ask anything else of you! I forbid you to mention him to me ever again."

She was a fine one to be outraged.

I pulled her in front of the tarnished mirror above the sideboard.

"Take a good look, Germaine. You're pretty; all you need is a proper haircut from a proper hair stylist and you'd be sensational. But instead of taking advantage of your youth and beauty you're skulking in this rat hole! You're fading away in

54

this shop, in this dead town! And you're not doing anything for yourself with those ridiculous clothes you wear—they're more provincial than the miserable high street out there! You're tossed back and forth between the slaps of one sick man and the embraces of another! Your precious secret life consists of shaving a hundred francs off the price of a steak in order to allow an arsehole to vegetate! That's what disgusts me. Roll on the time that your looks are as dull as your existence, so that no one's interested in you any more. At this rate, by the way, that won't be long."

I left her and went into the shop to mug up on the prices for funerals. The photographs of coffins made me feel pity. To think that I was going to extol the virtues of this junk to a guy, to try to tempt him with these corpse boxes. A real challenge!

Suddenly a slight sound coming from the bedroom made me stop and listen. A sound of stifled sobs. I got up and, with some hesitation, went to her. She was lying prone on her bed, weeping, her face hidden in the crook of her arm.

She was beautiful in her sorrow. In throwing herself on the bed she had, without noticing, hitched up a corner of her dressing gown and I could see a sensational leg, a firm calf whose warmth and velvety touch I could sense.

An immense compassion drew me towards her. This was serious: I loved her… I wanted her as well.

I knelt on the bed and stroked her ash-blonde hair. She pulled herself away.

"Leave me alone!" she cried through her tears.

I made her lift her head and gazed with love on her dear tear-streaked face.

"Germaine."

"Leave me alone!"

"Germaine, I know I've caused you pain, but I had to. It's my duty to open your eyes. No one has the right to let a girl like you drown in this foetid water! I'd also like to say that I love you. Oh, it's happened to me before, of course it has, but never this strong, never this fast. I… I'd do anything for you. There it is then! It's stupid to be forced to say shameful things like that, but it's too much for me, I can't keep them in."

She didn't move. She was looking attentive now. I leant forwards a little and furtively planted a kiss on her tear-stained lips. She didn't push me away, but did not return my kiss either.

I left the room, taking with me the salty taste of her sorrow.

Then I went and sold the butcher a stupendous coffin lined with silk, which would have made someone who loved comfort positively want to die!

5

Two days went by without incident. I was getting to grips with my new existence, selling funeral stuff at the homes of the deceased, even helping to place the "clients" in their coffins and transporting them to the church in old Corbain's ageing motorized hearse. I told myself this job wasn't right for me and that I mustn't let myself be anaesthetized by life in the provinces, but I had been through some difficult years and it felt good to be carried along on the easy gloom of those spring days.

The provinces are an opiate. The air there tastes sweet and life has a different texture than it has in Paris. It is denser, heavier, richer in meaning.

The undertaker was pleased with me. I was continuing to sell his premium products with an energy which left the more or less grief-stricken families I visited speechless.

Yes, those were two neutral and restful days. I took my midday meal in the boss's dining room. Germaine was a good cook and I enjoyed tasting her dishes, watching her the while.

Since I had kissed her, she barely spoke to me any more. There was something distant in her manner. I could see she regretted the scene between us. Her precious pride was rebelling, and she felt remorse about Maurice.

As for Castain, I was increasingly in his good books and he showed how pleased he was by noisy demonstrations and stupendous promises. According to him I had been conceived and put on this earth to sell coffins. Deep down he wasn't such a bad bastard. He had a nasty temper, like everyone with stomach problems, and he despised the wife he had married in… unusual circumstances. But I found him tolerable, at least where I was concerned.

It was on the evening of the third day that the drama was unleashed. We had taken a body to the chapel of rest and were on our way back to the shop. Castain was telling me about his military service and getting sentimental about it, of course. A newspaper seller went past, or rather *the* newspaper seller, because there was only one in the small town. The undertaker bought an evening paper. It was a local publication, produced in the regional capital, which came out three times a week.

Like all inhabitants of small towns, he was very attached to his newspaper. He stopped to read the headlines on the front page. I took the opportunity to light a cigarette. I breathed out some blue smoke and through the fleeting cloud I saw the colour drain from his face.

He stood still, speechless, mouth half-open in surprise.

"Something not quite right?" I asked solicitously.

But he didn't reply. I don't think my question had even got as far as his brain. He started walking again, in a jerky fashion. I had already noticed that when he was upset he had a nervous tic, which made him move his head up and down like those toy animals with articulated joints.

It was alarming now; you'd have thought he was nodding approval to people some distance away.

I would have liked to look at the front page of the rag which had thrown him into such a state of agitation, but he was clutching it in his right hand, like a pair of gloves. All I could do was follow him, and that wasn't easy: he was almost running.

Rue Haute at last, and the business. He burst into the shop, crying in a voice he could barely control, "Germaine!"

She appeared. That evening—I remember it very well— she was wearing for the first time a blue dress with a small yellow and grey print, slightly less ridiculous than the others.

"Oh, there you are," she murmured.

But her smile was short-lived.

"I know why you were so keen on going to Pont-de-l'Air!"

Fear flashed into Germaine's eyes. She gave herself away immediately by the way she recoiled.

"So," Castain began, "*he* had come back, eh?"

"But…"

He slapped her. I leapt forwards and seized him by the arm.

"No," I cried. "Not that!"

He tore himself free and ignored my intervention entirely. He was brandishing the newspaper he had just bought.

"When you went to the market over there it was to be with him! Come on, admit it!"

She didn't answer, but her very silence was the most positive of admissions.

"Slut! Bitch! Whore!"

I felt at the outer limit of anger, but told myself that a husband who's been cheated on does have the right to call his wife those names, and I clenched my fists, trying to calm down. One thing was nagging at me. I wondered how Castain had found out from the regional paper that his wife's lover was living in the area.

"Admit it!" yelled the undertaker. "Admit it, you slut! You were seeing that lout. Admit it before I do something you'll regret."

He was focused on his wife's lips. Impelled by a flame of masochism he was watching out for the confession that would hurt him, would strike him in the heart, in his pride…

"Will you admit it! Will you confess you were sleeping with *him* again? I want to hear you say it."

Tired out, drunk with fear, she nodded.

She seemed to be in a state of prostration bordering on a trance.

"Yes, Achille, I've seen him…"

His initial reflex was that of a wretched man proved right. He gave a strange little moan and let his arms drop down by his sides.

"So it's true?" he stuttered. "It's true!"

She nodded, seemingly mesmerized by the danger hanging over her.

The crumpled newspaper slipped from Castain's hand. With a weary sigh he bent down and took hold of it, for all the world as if it were a 200-pound weight. He spread it out.

"Good," he murmured, his voice suddenly very soft. "Fine, good, well now, look: he's dead."

That had the strangest effect on me. The news struck me on the head and set my thoughts chasing after one another like the horses on a merry-go-round. And, just like those horses, my thoughts couldn't catch up with one another.

"Dead," gasped Germaine.

He wanted to shout it, only it lodged in his throat. All he could get out was a sort of cavernous rattle.

"Yes, dead. He committed suicide, do you understand? He'd had enough of you! He's cleared off again, but this time it's for good! You'll never see him again, never! Ah! Serves him right!"

I thought he was going mad. Germaine took the paper out of his hands and he made no attempt to stop her. I moved closer to her to read it. It was on the front page, over two columns.

IN PONT-DE-L'AIR A SUICIDAL MAN DOES AWAY
WITH HIMSELF BY SLITTING HIS WRISTS!

The article began like this:

A young photographer from one of the region's old-established families, Maurice Thuillier, was discovered by his landlady this morning lying in a pool of blood. The unfortunate—who suffered from an incurable illness all his life—had killed himself by slitting the veins in his wrists.

Near to the body, a pile of burnt photographic prints was found, proving that the suicide destroyed certain documents before his death.

This last paragraph chilled me. It proved beyond doubt that I had just killed a man. Absolutely. It was I who had driven Thuillier to suicide, by pressing the button on his Rolleiflex. I could see quite clearly what had happened. When he had developed the photographs I had kindly taken, his illness had been revealed to him. Appalled, downcast by the truths I had flung in his face, he had chosen to end it once and for all. That is the courage of the weak. When they have taken enough blows, they go away. He had gone because he had understood that there was no place for him in this world. And I was the one who had made him see this hideous truth.

I wasn't proud… and yet this outcome seemed to me par for the course. We live in a ferocious universe where weaklings like Maurice have no place.

Castain was terrible to behold. His teeth were bared, and his lips were pulled back in the rictus of a mad dog. As for Germaine, she was breathing fast. Big tears were running down her cheeks. The silence which had set in around us was intolerable. I was searching for something to say to break it but could find nothing. Inside me there was a desert.

At long last Castain stirred himself. He looked up at Germaine and went for her.

He was slapping her, laying into her with his fists, kicking her… he truly was mad. Before I could intervene, Germaine's face was bloodied. This caused me a strange sort of pain. Seizing Castain by the arm, I landed a sharp hook on his cheekbone. He reeled and, drunk with fury, murder in his eyes, growled, "What the—?"

By way of answer he earned a mighty series of punches in the mouth. He crumpled.

"I can't bear to see anyone hit a woman, Castain… no matter what she's done, you don't have the right to thump her. It's not worthy of a man."

He knelt down, gasping. A cut had opened on his cheekbone and his left eye was swelling up like a balloon.

"What are you getting involved for?" he croaked. "Clear off out of here! I don't want to set eyes on you again. Scram! Have you got that?"

He opened his wallet and took out a 5,000-franc note, which he threw in my face.

"Get out of here this instant! Right now, or I call the police."

I trampled the 5,000-franc note to pieces on the shop floor.

"OK, Monsieur Hearse, I'm out of here. I've seen enough of you and your top-rate stiffs."

I turned to Germaine. "You're not going to stay with this madman, are you?"

She gestured towards the door.

"Leave, it's better that way… None of this has anything to do with you, he's right."

Good God, that little provincial could be so timid!

I shrugged my shoulders. I was hurting inside. Hurting with sadness, hurting with pity…

"I'm bloody sick of being a man," I sighed.

And I left.

It was almost dark. People were on their way home, arguing. The nice thing about the provinces is that people there take the time to live.

I made my way to the Hôtel de la Gare, head burning, my fists bruised from the blows I'd administered to my boss.

I went up to my room to get my cases ready, and that was the moment I realized I was short of money. I had less than 500 francs left, which was clearly not enough to settle the hotel bill and buy my ticket home. I would have to phone my friend Fargeot to scrounge 10,000 francs from him. Even if he wired them through to me, I wouldn't have them before the next day.

Sighing, I lay down fully dressed on the bed to wait for dinner time.

In the shadows I saw Thuillier's face, covered in froth. I pictured his feverish eyes, his haughty lower lip.

For him it was over. Finally he had understood and withdrawn from the contest. I almost envied him. And then I thought of Germaine, who from now on would be left alone with her hateful little undertaker. For her too it was over. No more romance, no fond feelings, no secret life…

After all, that's what she'd wanted. What had I hoped?

You cannot change someone else's destiny. Each of us bears our own skin and thoughts along the furrows of Fate.

I didn't give a damn.

Castain would continue to beat her. More frequently even, as now he had right on his side and a brand-new excuse.

She would continue to suffer, to submit. She would fade and die like a plant killed off by unsuitable soil.

It was sad, but what could I do? She had told me herself: none of that had anything to do with me. It was dirty linen, completely alien to me. I didn't have to involve myself in the laundering.

Through the curtains at the window I could see the sulphurous light of a gas lamp in the square. And in the evening mist its green flame was flickering like the wings of a dying butterfly.

PART TWO

6

I think I must have dozed off in my melancholy. There was a soft knock at my door. As I recall I was in the middle of dreaming about vague, distressing things... I sat up.

"Come in!"

I expected to see the hotel maid appear, summoning me to dinner. But instead, it was Castain who entered.

He had a piece of sticking plaster on his cheekbone and his eye was half-closed.

He came in, grave, solemn, bewildered. The darkness had disorientated him. I could see him easily, however, as he was lit by the corridor light.

"The light switch is on the left," I pointed out.

He flicked it on, before shutting the door again and smiling at me.

"Why are you here?" I asked him harshly.

"You're a good man, Delange."

"That's not true, leave me in peace!"

"I know what I'm talking about. You're a good man and I'm not in the least angry with you for the dressing-down you gave me... Good God! You can hit hard!"

Where was he going with this? There was a crafty little glint in his good eye.

"Thanks for your absolution. It's always a pleasure. Now we have nothing further to say to each other."

He plonked himself down at the end of the bed.

"Yes we do. I've got a lot to say to you. You were present at a distressing scene…"

"Let's call it 'odious', I like to be precise in my choice of words!"

"All right, 'odious'. But you have to know what lies underneath it all."

I was sitting cross-legged, leaning against my pillow.

"Please don't go confiding in me, Castain. I have a horror of that. People's pasts are like big stones pulled up out of the ground: underneath they're swarming with all sorts of nasty black creepy-crawlies."

"But I'm keen to tell you that if my behaviour is difficult to excuse, then it may at least be explained."

"Good for you—it'll salve your conscience."

"Don't be unpleasant. Listen to me!"

In his present state, he needed to confess like a chap fainting in the Sahara needs water. Allowing him to get it out was doing him a service. He had been kind to me, after all. I let him spill his guts. Of course I got the story Germaine had already told me, only revised and edited from his own point of view. He portrayed himself as the hero. He was the man with the generous heart, the lover full of self-sacrifices, the one who sees the situation clearly, the one who clears the branches to make the path easier.

From all that, one thing emerged at any rate: he loved his wife. On those grounds he merited all my fellow-feeling, all my jealousy as well.

When he had finished rummaging through his personal dustbin a deep silence fell.

"There it is," he said, seeing I was doing nothing to break it. "What do you think about my situation?"

"I think that your situation is also your wife's situation, isn't it? You're kicking up a fuss for no good reason. How old are you, Castain?"

"Fifty-two."

"And she's…?"

"Twenty-eight."

"Right, you can do subtraction can't you? That'll prove to you that you could be her father. Instead of getting worked up about it, you'd do better to act in a way that's worthy of the experience you've had."

"But I love her!"

"That's just it. Let's examine the facts. When she was a young girl, your wife was seduced by a boy her own age— that's what usually happens, isn't it?"

"Yes."

"Excellent. You may perhaps have demonstrated generosity in marrying her, but that did at least allow you to attain a girl who was logically beyond your reach. From what I've seen of your life together, instead of cherishing her you treat her like a servant, and then you're surprised to find out she's returned to her youthful errors? If you want my opinion, my friend, you've only got what you deserve."

"Steady on."

"If I were you, at this point I would take advantage of the drama to change my strategy; I would caress her, I'd be a friend to her, if you know what that means?"

"I see, yes."

"So much the better! In time, she'll forget this vile past. The fact that she's stayed with you in spite of the young man's return proves that she's attached to you."

His one eye began to shine, full of hope.

"Do you believe that?"

"Just think about it."

"Yes, it's just…"

"Then act accordingly and stop beating her!"

He held out his nasty, smooth, yellowish hand.

"Thank you, Delange…"

"Don't mention it. I'm holding surgery today."

"Of course our dust-up is all forgotten, isn't it? You'll come back to the business?"

"Never!"

"Oh yes."

"No! Really, Monsieur Castain, you do realize I'm out of my element here? I need a more active life… I love travel, I love Paris!"

I will never forget the sadness on his face.

"You can't do that to us, Delange! We can't suddenly be left on our own here, just the two of us, Germaine and me. Heal us!"

I found that touching. Besides, all I wanted was to see her again…

"Agreed."

For two or three days, I can tell you, life at the funeral director's was not pleasant. It felt more like being in a tomb than in a place of business. My hosts spoke only when it was strictly necessary and avoided looking at each other. Germaine was like a dog that's been beaten. She dragged herself from the kitchen to the dining room like a weary shadow, and whenever our eyes met she would quickly look away.

I sensed that this state of affairs could not continue for very long. It was enough to drive you mad. I carried on visiting bereaved families, extolling the charms of a big funeral… this was becoming routine. I was now known in the area. Women looked fondly at me and men would buy me a drink at the first opportunity.

One evening, as I was leaving the shop, Castain said to me, "I'll go with you as far as the end of the road, to get some air. I've been doing the accounts all day and my head is bursting."

We walked in silence for a moment before he began: "Well, what do you think?"

I wrinkled my nose.

"Umm, not very much."

"Quite so! Yet I'm doing what I can, I'm speaking kindly to her. I even told her I forgave her…"

"And what did she say?"

"It was as if she hadn't heard me! She doesn't want to know."

"She'll get over it."

"Do you think so? It's making me ill."

I looked at him. It was true, he didn't appear at all well. His skin was more yellow than usual and he had huge grey rings under his eyes. The man was being worn away by illness… I would have sworn he had cancer or some filth of that sort.

"You look very ill, Monsieur Castain. You ought to see your doctor."

That hit home. He ran his horrid bony hand over his face, like a blind person trying to identify some object. He seemed to be having difficulty in recognizing himself.

"Yes, my stomach's not great. I've had problems for years. But at the moment, with all this worry... Right, I'll go tomorrow."

He did in fact go the next day. His doctor was an old fellow I had come to know by sight and who smelt like a dead rat. This doctor had attended the births of everyone in the area and was at least eighty. People were wondering what he was waiting for, before handing on his practice to someone younger. Of course, all the locals placed their trust in him. He was still treating angina with lemon juice, and cases of pleurisy with poultices, but there were no more deaths here than elsewhere for all that.

We were at the table, Germaine and I, nibbling radishes and not looking at each other, when Castain came back from his consultation, worried.

"Well?" I asked.

He couldn't have told his wife he was going to the doctor's as she seemed surprised when he said:

"Boileau's concerned. He's advising me to go to Paris, to the Hôtel-Dieu."

"Then you must go."

It scared him. He dreaded finding out something bad.

"Next week."

"Why wait?"

"No, next week."

We sat down at the table. He took some bismuth, looking mournful. Germaine had slumped back into her apathy. The more I looked at her, the more I desired her. My love for her was like burning embers which smoulder for a long time before a draft catches them and they become an inferno. As I watched them both, I realized Castain was *de trop* and that if he were to disappear there would be no one between her and me.

She didn't love me, she was too preoccupied by her recent grief, but that was precisely what excited me. I wanted to conquer her. Castain's yellowish complexion allowed the highest of hopes. I tried in vain to drive away the terrible thought. It recurred relentlessly, more fully formed each time: if he had cancer he would croak, little by little. And I…

No, that was decidedly too horrible.

"You need to go immediately, Monsieur Castain. Take the train tomorrow. You must… with every hour that goes by…"

He gestured agreement.

"Yes, tomorrow, that's agreed, Blaise. Tomorrow, once and for all."

When I pushed open the shop door the next morning, he had already left. There was a note for me on the desk:

> Blaise
>
> I've taken your advice. Nothing in particular today. Please answer this correspondence. See you this evening.
>
> A.C.

I was ill at ease knowing I was alone in the house with Germaine. I went through to the dining room. She wasn't there. However, I could hear her moving about in the bedroom. I knocked on the door. Not getting an answer, I went in.

Germaine was wearing her dreadful little black suit and her white blouse. She was piling lingerie into a cheap cardboard suitcase.

I went over to her.

"What are you doing, Germaine?"

"You can see for yourself!"

"You're leaving?"

"Yes."

"For where?"

"I've no idea and that's the least of my worries!"

"Why are you going?"

"Why do prisoners saw through their prison bars?"

"There's nothing to keep you here any more, is that it?"

"No, nothing."

The two words came out in a squeak and tears sprang from her periwinkle-blue eyes.

"And you're taking advantage of the fact that the chief warder is away to make a run for it?"

"What difference does it make to you?"

"You've merely forgotten one thing, Germaine."

She stared at me curiously. Then, confronted with my no doubt eloquent expression, she shook her head:

"It's true, you're in love with me."

"Not in love, I love you, subtle difference."

"Why should that matter to me since I don't love you?"

"Thank you for your honesty!"

"Would a lie on my part be preferable, do you think?"

"Certainly not."

"Then?"

"Then nothing… except that I'm not going to let you leave."

"Really?"

"Really! It would be folly, and when I can prevent my fellow men from committing foolish acts, I intervene."

She looked me up and down as if to challenge me.

"There are moments when even Good Samaritans are very annoying!"

"I'm sorry to annoy you, but you're not leaving."

"At least explain yourself! And don't hide behind some hypocritical excuse."

"Germaine, I'm telling you again, I love you with all my strength. You're the only reason I stayed here. I'm not going to let you run away. There, that's clear. No more to be said."

She shrugged and went back to packing her suitcase. I felt slightly stupid. If she persisted in trying to leave, then I wasn't about to tie her up while waiting for Castain's return. I had never before found myself in such an awkward situation.

Germaine continued packing her underwear. The lace, the white silk slips made my cheeks grow hot.

When the case was ready, she slammed down the lid and clicked both locks shut. Then she took a coat from the wardrobe, threw it round her shoulders and picked up her luggage. This was it. The crucial moment had arrived.

I turned the key in the lock.

"No funny business, Germaine, you are not leaving here!"

She looked me straight in the eye. I could gauge how determined she was from the intensity of her stare.

"Let me past or I'll shout for help."

"You are not leaving this room!"

She reached for the lock. I blocked her path.

"Don't be ridiculous, Germaine. Don't make me lay hands on you."

"Get out of my way or I'll shout, I won't warn you again."

She was scarlet.

Suddenly she dropped her suitcase and ran to the bedroom window. I sprang the width of the bed and put my arm round her just as she grabbed the window latch. I snatched her away from the window. She was struggling, kicking, letting out little shrieks. I had no intention of letting go of her. Her quivering body was spreading an intense heat to mine. As we struggled we bumped into the bed and fell on top of each other. My face found itself above hers.

I kissed her abruptly, so suddenly that she had no time to turn her mouth away. Our teeth met noisily, my lip burst and instantly I tasted blood in my mouth. She tried to cry out, opening her mouth, I bit back that cry. I don't remember the details very well after that... I know she suddenly stopped struggling. Yes, she lay motionless on the bedcover. With furious and precise movements I ripped apart the black suit. There were pieces of it all over the bedroom; we gathered them up, in silence, afterwards, once I had taken her.

7

We said nothing for a long time, thunderstruck by the intense happiness which had descended on us without any warning. We were stupefied. Circumstances had just turned us into lovers and, frankly, we weren't prepared for that.

I looked at her anxiously. She was lying full-length on the bed, hands behind her head, gazing at the ceiling.

"Germaine…"

She moved her chin very slightly.

"Are you angry with me, my love?"

Why do two people who have just made love feel the need to use terms of endearment? That's one of the mysteries of love—and there are many others.

"Tell me, are you angry with me?"

"Why would I be angry with you?"

"Well… when a woman doesn't love a man, and that man takes her by force, I would think her indifference turns to hatred."

"I don't hate you, Blaise, perhaps I even love you… Yes, that must be it. I liked you, and now I think I love you. Only it's not like anything I've ever known. It's completely different. You wouldn't understand!"

I didn't need to understand. Her words brought me a new happiness, even more dazzling than before.

"Don't say any more, Germaine. Why try to define what we're feeling? Isn't the most important thing that we make each other happy and that we don't want to part?"

"I don't know."

"I do."

The day went by gently, like a ray of sunlight stealing across a room. We repeated the exercise several times, and each time we became more passionate.

When Castain returned from Paris that evening our faces bore the ravages of our desire, something which would certainly have attracted his attention if he hadn't been so happy.

"It's nothing serious!" he said triumphantly as he stepped into the shop. "The beginnings of an ulcer, and liver troubles, that's all!"

He insisted that I dine with them. He spent the whole evening giving us chapter and verse on his internal organs with a wealth of clinical detail that got on my nerves.

Dare I confess? I was cruelly disappointed. I had made a firm decision now: Germaine would be mine alone. Since the miserable man had a future ahead of him, we would leave.

"The nuisance," he concluded, "is that I'll have to go to Paris for treatment every week... Well, I'm counting on you, Blaise."

I tried to keep any trace of irony out of my reply: "You can count on me, Monsieur Castain."

For two days I could find no opportunity to be alone with Germaine. I was dying of suppressed desire. When I saw her going about the house I had to restrain myself from taking her in my arms... I think that if the undertaker had made a move, I would have smashed a carafe over his head.

Finally, two days after his trip to Paris, he was occupied with a service and we were able to… be together truly, the pair of us.

Castain's puny figure, more ridiculous than ever in his uniform, which made him look as if he was impersonating a student at the prestigious École Polytechnique, hadn't even turned the corner of the street before I'd locked the shop door and gone to Germaine in the bedroom. We didn't say a single word. We were trembling with impatience. That was the most furtive and powerful of our embraces, I think.

Afterwards I went back into the shop and waited for her to join me. She did come, drawn by the irresistible need we had for each other.

"Germaine, when will we go away?"

She gave a start.

"Go away?"

"You can't think we're going to go on making love in the odd half-hour behind his back for ever!"

"I don't want to leave, Blaise."

I brought my fist down hard on the desk, furious.

"Good God, there it is, the fickleness of women. Two days ago I had to assault you in order to stop you from running away, and now you're refusing?"

"Because two days ago I was going on my own."

"Go on, explain yourself—I don't understand the subtlety of that distinction."

"I don't understand it either, Blaise, but I can tell it exists. The other day I was leaving to be with a memory. In my eyes I retained all my honour."

She certainly had a way of expressing herself. I smiled.

"Honour! Do you know what that is?"

"Better than a man, no doubt, even though it's supposed to be a male speciality. If I were to leave now I would be a slut running off with her husband's employee."

"Do other people's opinions bother you?"

"No, but my own does."

I sensed she was not to be moved, so I didn't insist, but a great sadness took away all my joie de vivre.

Since receiving the news that he might live to be a hundred, Castain had decidedly regained his self-assurance, and was beginning to ignore his good resolutions. One morning I arrived at work to find Germaine with one cheek on fire. Guessing that her chimpanzee had slapped her, I gestured my question. She answered yes. Her eyes were burning with hatred.

Castain was whistling, ill at ease. I think he was afraid of me. He feared I might notice the situation and chastise him again. So he instructed me to get off to a new client pronto.

I gritted my teeth and obeyed, anxious to avoid a scene. I didn't want to risk losing Germaine now; if he had shown me the door and she had refused to follow, that's exactly what would have happened. Because of her stubbornness in not wanting to do anything wrong our love was hanging by a thread.

So I grasped the briefcase with the samples and set off for the address I'd been given.

The deceased I was going to see was a wealthy property dealer in the town. He had just died following a short illness, at the very moment he was about to be divorced in order to "start a new life".

His widow was in her forties, with a dress sense eccentric for this region. She was foreign, I think Romanian, and spoke with an Eastern European accent which must have seen quite a few doors in the local area closed to her.

She received me in an outlandish black dress with flounces, which suggested an evening at Maxim's rather than a bereavement.

In robust language she explained that the Good Lord had punished her fickle husband; that there was an immanent justice in which she had blind faith, and told me to give the deceased an "original" funeral: that was the word she used.

She was hesitating between a bare coffin to be carried on men's shoulders or an enormous catafalque on a gun carriage.

I used diplomacy to guide her back onto the path of reason and flogged her a service fit for a king, with a grand organ, draperies, sung Mass and chapel of rest.

Madame Crémant—that was the customer's name— insisted that the body be placed in the coffin as quickly as possible and taken to the church; no doubt she was of the view that it made the house look "untidy".

I promised her everything she wanted and left, pleased, in spite of my preoccupations, to have done a good piece of business.

The next morning, Castain asked me to help him put the property dealer in the coffin, as his employee trained for this task was unavailable. We went to the dead man's house with the hearse, equipped with a posh casket. The police commissioner had been waiting for us there for a while. Our arrival relieved him of the eccentric widow, who was taking him to task. We requested she leave us to our work, and shut ourselves up in the room where the body lay.

Once we had put the casket on the floor, we went over to the dead man's bed. At that point Castain gave a growl of displeasure and took me aside.

"You've done something stupid, my poor Delange."

"Something stupid?"

"Where the measurements are concerned. Can't you see that this casket is much too large for Monsieur Crémant? You could fit two of him in there."

However, we proceeded to place him in the coffin, screwed on the lid and took the deceased to the church once we'd said farewell to the commissioner.

Mass had just finished and the building was deserted. It was stormy that day. The sky was crushing the town under bloated grey clouds. In the church, and especially in the small chapel where the bier had been prepared, there floated an underwater half-light. The flowers, already in place, were exuding a heady scent.

Castain got to work. He was settling his client in the chapel the way an assiduous hotelier settles his guests into their rooms.

"What are you thinking about?" he asked peremptorily.

He was frowning, his thin eyebrows forming a single horizontal line.

I didn't answer. How could I? I was thinking of his remark shortly before about the coffin's over-ample dimensions: "You could fit two of him in there."

He was looking me up and down, hands on hips, haughty, displeased, for reasons I could not fathom. And I was calculating his measurements, my eye suddenly precise. I was telling myself that he was smaller than the dead man… telling myself he would be good company for the property dealer. Telling myself that this was a unique opportunity, a dreamt-of, unexpected and fabulous opportunity to get him out of our way for ever!

The silence in the church was extraordinarily heavy.

"What's the matter with you?" he muttered.

His ugly face, his unpleasant voice, his petty aggression made me want to scream.

I shifted my weight to get some power into my swing, then, before he had a chance to foresee what I was about to do, I floored him with a fearsome hook to the chin.

He crumpled silently into the flowers, seriously dazed. His eyes rolled. I seized the black sheet folded into eight which we were about to spread over the coffin, laid it on his head and threw myself down on top of it… I must have remained in that pose for an eternity. If anyone had come in I'd have been caught like a rat in a trap. What possible explanation could there be for a position like that? But, as I said before, the church was deserted.

Castain moved his hands feebly for a while, before his fingers curled over and he was still; I could feel he was limp beneath the black cloth. I knelt down, removed the sheet from his face and knew he was dead. A strange feeling of release filled my chest. I felt calm, at peace. I pushed the corpse under the trestle supporting the coffin and covered it with the heavy black drapery. Then I breathed in the sugary scent of the flowers... I only vaguely understood what had just happened and I knew it would be a long time before I could take it in. I walked out casually to fetch our crank-handle screwdriver from the hearse parked outside the church. Hiding it under my jacket, I returned to the chapel.

The rest isn't very clear in my memory... I know I unscrewed the lid of the coffin, unfolded the shroud wrapped round the "client", then hoisted Castain into the coffin and replaced the lid. I had a moment of blind panic when the lid wouldn't go back into place. I don't wish to go into the macabre details but I have to admit that I put the two corpses side on, face to face, and then did what one does with an overfull trunk: I sat down on the lid. The screws bit into the holes. Using all my strength to turn the handle, I screwed the lid down all the way. I was happy to be able to get the coffin lid back on. It was closing for ever on the past.

On Germaine's past at least, the only one which interested me.

8

When I came out of the church there was no one in sight. I had benefited, if I may put it like that, from extremely favourable circumstances. I sat at the wheel of the hearse and started the motor.

Now I was confronted with a fait accompli—oh how "accompli"! God was my witness that it wasn't premeditated. I believe that in committing this murder in the church I had obeyed a sort of strange prompting. Everything had played a role in my action: the half-light, the heady perfume of the flowers, Castain's aggressive attitude... I can still see him there, standing square on his spindly little legs, asking me what I was thinking about. Above all, the remark he'd made at Crémant's house had in some mysterious way brought about the irrevocable.

Without trying to, I had just committed what was surely a perfect murder. But life went on, and Castain's disappearance was not going to go unnoticed.

As I steered the small black hearse through the narrow streets of the town I was constructing a plan of action. I remembered that my boss had intended to catch the 11.35 train to Paris. That afternoon, in fact, he had an appointment with the specialist who was to start treatment for his ulcerating stomach.

I stopped the vehicle in front of the shop. I got out. I was resolved to say nothing to Germaine. For her, above all, I'd have to put on a good performance.

I went in and washed my hands in the kitchen. She was peeling vegetables for the midday meal.

"Horrible job," I said. "I'm fed up with moving corpses about. Hasn't Achille come back?"

"Isn't he with you?"

"No, he left suddenly, saying that he'd just met a friend who was driving to Paris and he wanted to take the opportunity of going with him… I thought he'd come in to get changed?"

"He hasn't been."

"Ah."

That was all for the day. We had our meal and finished up in the bedroom. I wasn't really clear on where Germaine was, emotionally speaking. Was she still thinking about Maurice Thuillier? Was she suffering because of his dramatic death? Was she tormented by the past? All worrying questions I asked myself without daring to put them to her. In any case, on the physical side she really threw herself into it. Each of our embraces exceeded the one before. That girl had certainly never known a man who was able to satisfy her physically.

In the afternoon I was busy with the funeral for… Crémant. I finalized the details for the ceremony, which was to take place the following day. Then in the evening, as usual, I returned to the hotel.

I went to bed as soon as dinner was out of the way and tried to read a book, but I must have started the first sentence fifteen times over without being able to take in the meaning of the characters on the page.

Nevertheless, I left the light on and fell asleep very quickly. But in the middle of the night, the electricity disturbed me and dragged me out of sleep. I was bathed in sweat. A silent anguish was chewing at me. I drank a little water from the washbasin; it tasted of rust. My clothes, on the chair, smelt of corpses... I was unspeakably dejected. In the space of a few days I had caused the deaths of two people, for the love of a woman. I had become a killer and I was accepting it without a murmur, without noticing the slightest difference with "before". By associating with the dead of the area I had come to understand that they were not frightening. They had changed their state, that was all. Castain, too, had changed his state.

I pulled the switch that hung above the bed. Darkness gripped me round the throat. Then my eyes grew accustomed to it and it stopped being dark. The rectangle of the window, with the whitish patch of the curtains and the flame of the distant gas lamp... the yellow shaft of light under the door... vague reflections in the dressing-table mirror, all of that belonged to the light. All this gave me my strength back, gave me confidence. I had to take advantage of the light, since it belongs only to the living.

To say that worry was gnawing away at Germaine the next day would be an exaggeration. What she felt was more akin to surprise. This was the first time that Castain had stayed away overnight. She thought he had missed his train the day before, even that he had done a bunk, but she was astonished that he hadn't telephoned to reassure her.

We contemplated the possibility of an accident. That didn't upset her in the least. She hated her husband sufficiently to accept the idea of his death without flinching.

"We ought to telephone the station," I suggested.

The strangest thing was that I was taken in by my own pretence. I really did have the impression that Castain had gone away and that I was waiting for him. Yes: I was waiting for him!

I phoned the station to find out when the next train from Paris would arrive. The employee replied that one had just come in and that there wouldn't be another until the middle of the afternoon. I asked him if Monsieur Castain had been seen at the station. He told me he had not. Had he asserted the opposite, I think I would have believed him.

Germaine was at a loss.

"What do you think all this means, Blaise?"

I shrugged my shoulders.

"I don't know… It seems to me that if he'd had an accident you would already have been informed. He must have had identification on him, mustn't he?"

"What if he'd fallen from the train?"

"But he was going with a friend."

"I wonder what could have made him decide to do that. He's a real scaredy-cat and frightened of car journeys."

She shrugged her shoulders.

"Well, we'll see," she pronounced. "The trouble is there won't be anyone in the shop."

"Why?"

"Because I'm going to Crémant's funeral."

I couldn't help crying out: "You?"

"Yes. He was a great friend of my father's and I went to school with his daughter."

"I see. All right."

She went to get ready. Meanwhile I phoned the usual pall-bearers to tell them to do what was necessary, as the boss wasn't there.

I was troubled. I was uneasy about conducting the burial service. It wasn't my kind of thing and I knew nothing about the protocol.

I took the hearse to go to my hotel and put on a dark navy-blue suit; with a white shirt and black tie, it would do…

I can still see us, Germaine and me, with the silent throng of the funeral procession.

I was walking to the side of the column of mourners, like a sheepdog escorting its flock. I felt vaguely ridiculous, which took my mind off my anxiety somewhat.

Germaine had taken her place with the women. She was wearing a violet dress and a black cloth coat. They showed off her blonde hair and olive complexion. I loved her figure, her sculpted curves, her long, shapely legs… Later, when everything had quietened down, I would dress her like a model. I would teach her how to put on make-up, how to carry herself.

She had no inkling, as she walked pensively in the slow-moving crowd, that she was following her husband's mortal remains. Only I knew that.

When they had lifted the coffin, one of the bearers had whispered in my ear: "He weighs as much as a cow, that one."

That had made me shiver. I'd murmured in an offhand tone, "It's more the lead lining inside the coffin… His wife's idea."

Now I just wanted it all to be over.

During the church service, which was endless, I had cursed myself for advising Madame Crémant to have such an elaborate one. And afterwards the way to the cemetery had seemed horrendously long.

Two men in one coffin! I imagined the two dead men piled into this wooden casket for eternity. They had spent their lives in different social circles, with different aspirations, and the strangeness of Fate had united them for ever in the same tomb.

We reached the cemetery at last. The bearers laid the coffin on the ground. The gravediggers were waiting near to a gaping lair. Then came the succession of mourners to sprinkle holy water. Next, the relatives took up their positions at the cemetery entrance to shake hands. That was a royal chore which would never fall to Germaine.

Soon I was alone by the pit, with the gravediggers. They passed the cords under the casket and lowered it into the grave, where two other coffins already lay.

I said a secret prayer that Castain would rest in peace, and that I would too.

From now on, Germaine had no one but me. The world was ours. As I was leaving the cemetery the sun showed its pale face through the clouds. I saw in it something like a promise and, who knows, perhaps an absolution.

9

On the evening of that same day, at my behest, Germaine informed the police of her husband's disappearance. It was really the next day, however, before it became a concern in the area.

News travels fast in these backwaters. In a matter of hours, a powder trail had been lit; the entire county knew that its undertaker had disappeared from circulation. The shop was filled with people coming to see what was going on, each of them voicing theories, every one of which was more bizarre than the one before. Germaine, like the rest, went off into speculation.

"I think I can be fairly sure that he didn't have a mistress," she confided. "And even if he were having an affair, he would never have left. He'd sooner have thrown me out: his business was his whole life!"

I tried to offer a valid solution to the problem.

"I suppose, lately, he'd been very sad about you… Suppose he'd experienced a spell of depression?"

"Him, kill himself? You must be joking! Don't you remember he was overjoyed when the doctors assured him he didn't have anything very serious?"

The police pulled out all the stops, of course. The commissioner, whom I already knew, made endless phone calls to the Paris hospitals, the morgue, the organizations for missing persons and for their families trying to find them.

It was an eventful week. An officer from the crime division came and asked us a thousand questions. I'd made a mistake in inventing the story of Castain travelling to Paris with a friend. The police left no stone unturned in the area to find out who had gone to the capital that day. A man of Castain's acquaintance, who sold pigs wholesale, was questioned for hours purely because he had gone to Paris that morning. The doctor in Paris was contacted and stated, of course, that his patient had not kept his appointment. When asked if the businessman's illness was benign, he replied that it was precisely for further tests that Castain had arranged the consultation. It was a real mystery. But as a heap of people go missing every day, in France and elsewhere, the police put the matter on the back-burner and Germaine and I were left on our own.

We were legally responsible for making a decision concerning the shop, and after examining the situation closely we decided to keep trading for the time being. After all, Castain might well reappear (other people were justified in thinking that, at least), and Germaine had no authority to stop managing her husband's business.

I therefore asked the head bearer to be in charge of the ceremonies, and life, for what it was worth, went on. As in the past, I continued to have my midday meal at Germaine's and go back to my hotel when evening came. What else could I do?

There was still talk of the mystery, but the prevailing theory was that of suicide. People thought that Castain, knowing he was ill and noticing that I was deceiving him with his wife—because there was no doubt about this among the local gossips—had done away with himself. They had dragged the rivers, searched the wells, the septic tanks, the ponds, the thickets… Everyone expected someone to stumble across the body sooner or later.

This irksome life oppressed me even more than when Castain was alive. We sank into a strange kind of torpor which took the zest out of our love. You have to understand: we no longer dared to make love because of the sword of Damocles hanging over our embraces. Every time we heard the shop door open, from the bedroom or the dining room, Germaine would grow as pale as wax and close her eyes in a near-faint. At those moments I wanted to tell her the truth, but knowing how unbending she was I was not unaware that if I had the misfortune to confess my crime to her, she would refuse ever to see me again.

One evening, as I was getting ready to leave her and return to the Hôtel de la Gare, I sat down on the corner of the desk.

"Germaine, listen, I've had enough of this existence."

"It's no fun for me either."

"Then let's stop being idiots, and go away! You'll look for a manager and we'll go and live what I call 'our life'."

"But…"

"Please, don't argue. Just think it through a little. And look things in the face, as they say. One of two things: either Castain is dead, or he isn't. If he is, you may do as you please and do whatever you like with yourself, and to hell with what other people say…"

I paused slightly. This was difficult to say without betraying emotion.

"If he's alive…"

She looked at me; her eyes had an indefinable little glint that came and went. Yes, they were the eyes of someone with a strong ulterior motive who is trying not to let it show.

"If he's alive?" she prompted.

"If he's alive, Germaine, then he's left you, in which case you're likewise free, do you understand? In either case, you win."

She didn't answer. I saw her floundering in a mass of bizarre considerations.

"So, what do you suggest?"

I wiped my brow with the back of my hand. I thought it was covered in sweat, but no, on the contrary, it was icy. She was giving in, I was winning.

As you can imagine, I had planned it all out recently. I hardly slept any more, and you know as well as I do that insomnia is the best fertilizer for the imagination.

"Right. You'll say you're not able to look after the business on your own, OK?"

"Yes."

"You're going to find a manager."

"Then what?"

"As soon as you've found one, I'll leave here, lock stock and barrel. I'll go round and say goodbye to everyone, do you understand?"

"And then?"

She was snorting with impatience. Her nostrils were flaring.

"Three days later you'll come and join me in Paris."

Of course, the little provincial bourgeoise in her got the upper hand.

"But what will I say to people here?"

"Shit!" I thundered. "You'll say shit to those plebs! Make up any old thing if their gracious esteem means that much to you! How wonderful of you to be so attached to the gossip of a handful of yokels. If you care more about your social standing than my love, say so right now so I know where I stand."

"Don't be horrible, Blaise."

She thought for a while.

"And… if my husband comes back?"

"Then you send him postcards, in colour! How many times? Right is on your side. He's the one who left the marital home, isn't he?"

"Of course."

"About the management, give the guy who takes it on control of the business on a conditional basis; that way, if Castain comes back the replacement will have to disappear."

"As you wish, Blaise."

I took hold of her by the shoulders and gazed intently at her. I forgot myself in that wonderful blue… I placed my cheek against hers.

"So it's agreed, Germaine?"

"It's agreed, Blaise!"

"You'll join me?"

"I'll join you."

"You swear?"

"I swear."

"No regrets?"

"No regrets."

"Tell me…"

"What, my darling?"

"The other one?"

"Which other one?"

"You know quite well."

"Maurice?"

"Yes."

"Let's not speak about him, do you mind?"

"Just this once, to tell me… do you still love him?"

She shook her head.

With that denial I was with her all the way. Quite literally.

"Will you love me for ever, Germaine?"

"I need your love so badly, Blaise, that 'for ever' isn't long enough!"

PART THREE

10

Everything happened just as I'd planned, and three weeks later Germaine and I were finally living together in Paris.

I had turned up a little furnished studio in Montmartre, Rue Caulaincourt. The windows looked onto the street and we were able to breathe in the strange scent of the acacias, which was heightened by the spring.

During the few days in which I'd been waiting for my mistress, I had worried a great deal about money. Love is a wonderful thing, but not a dish you accompany with a glass of water, like an ice-cream dessert. If you're to savour it properly, material cares have to be banished... But I had no money and not the slightest idea of how to acquire any.

I wasn't too confident, I must admit, as I went to meet Germaine at the station. I had a few thousand francs left. After that, nothing: I was leaping into the unknown with a woman to look after.

She was delighted by Paris. When I saw her making her way through the crowds, on that bustling station platform, my heart started beating madly and seemed to burn.

I was suffocating with happiness. She came towards me, smiling, transformed, radiant, with her suitcase in her hand.

I took her luggage and kissed her, and we left the station arm in arm. We couldn't think of anything to say. The sun was magnificent, and the air so pure that just breathing it made you feel elated.

Our studio consisted of a living room and a little kitchen-cum-bathroom. Everywhere was painted straw-yellow. The furnishings were modern and the apartment benefited from large casement windows. It was a world away from the rathole in which Germaine had lived for so long.

"Do you like it?"

"It's marvellous: a real fairy story, darling."

She frowned.

"Just one thing… It must be madly expensive."

I hid my worries.

"You don't have to think about that, it's my domain."

"Not at all, I know you're not rich… Wait—"

She opened her suitcase and took out a small biscuit tin held closed by a thick rubber band.

"Here."

"What's this?"

"Have a look."

I took off the rubber band and opened the tin. It was full of gold Louis d'or. There were so many it didn't seem real.

"It's Castain's nest egg," she explained. "I found it in the cellar when I was tidying."

She became serious.

"That was what made me really realize he's dead."

"Why?"

"He loved gold. He would never have abandoned this heap of coins. Do you know how many there are?"

"No."

"Five hundred and forty… How much is that?"

I did a quick calculation.

"Almost two million."

"Then we're rich!"

"Do you think…"

"Well, look. Even if he came back he wouldn't be able to prosecute me. Theft from one's spouse is not recognized as a crime."

I thought of Thuillier. I had showered him with sarcasm, he had died because of my contempt, and here I was, taking his inheritance. I was letting myself be kept by a woman… I wanted to refuse the treasure but it brought us a well-being our love badly needed.

When I think about that period, I have to admit it was an exceptional time in my life. I introduced Germaine to Paris, I dressed her the way I wanted her to be dressed; she quickly became an elegant woman, with delightful outfits. I made appointments for her at the hair salons on the Champs-Élysées, I took her to fine restaurants, to the theatres, shopping… We hired a small car and went on excursions in the surrounding area: Versailles, Rambouillet, Montfort l'Amaury, Fontainebleau…

It was like a fabulous honeymoon.

What a joy it is for a man to be able to devote himself entirely to the woman he loves! She was my only occupation, my sole concern.

Absorbed in my new life, I no longer thought about what I had done. From now on, Castain was far away; the earth had swallowed him up. He was dissolving in its monstrous entrails and fading in our memories… I knew that after several years he would be declared dead, and once he'd been struck out of the official records Germaine would inherit his assets. Then we would take a little shop and live a happy life, sheltered from want.

One morning when we were still in bed, sleeping late as we did every day, an urgent ringing of the doorbell made us jump. I pulled on my dressing gown and went to the door. I thought my chest would burst. Standing on the threshold was the police commissioner who had been present at the house when Crémant was put into his coffin. He was smiling in a cordial, vaguely embarrassed fashion. He was an elderly officer who was serving out his final year in the provinces. Now, a few months off retirement, he bore the marks of a dreary life spent in offices where no mystery had ever shown its face.

He was waiting, hat in hand. He was a stocky man, whose bald head had a crown of thick grey curls like astrakhan. He had a frank expression and a smile studded with gold fillings.

"Good day, Monsieur Delange. I'm not disturbing you, I hope?"

I tried to get a grip on myself.

"Not at all."

"I'd like to see Madame Castain. This is where she lives, I think?"

"But… yes."

I stood aside to let him pass. There was no way of preventing him.

So he gained entrance to the studio. Germaine was still lying on the divan. She was wearing a gossamer-like nightdress through which her breasts were visible.

The commissioner greeted her without batting an eyelid, as if he were paying a polite visit to some posh salon.

"Forgive me for bothering you so early in the morning…"

I detected the hidden irony in his words; in fact, ten o'clock had just struck.

"Has there been a development?"

In her excitement she had sat down on the bed, heedless of the fact that her chest was practically bare.

"Maybe…"

It was lucky he wasn't looking at me, since he'd have noticed my face crumple completely. I automatically glanced into a mirror; I'd just aged ten years on the spot.

The policeman explained.

"We're told there's a man in Nantes whose description corresponds exactly to that of your husband. The individual in question is an amnesiac who was found on a train. He's in a psychiatric hospital and I think it would be good if… if you…"

My blood started circulating again.

"Very well, Monsieur le Commissaire, we'll go to Nantes this afternoon."

He turned to me.

"Yes, just in case. Personally, mind you, I don't believe this is your husband."

"Why?" Germaine asked.

He shook his head. His hand with its sausage-like fingers walked over his smooth skull.

"In my opinion, Madame Castain, your spouse is dead. I'm sorry to cause you sorrow…"

Still that veiled irony which was getting on my nerves.

He stood up.

"Good, that's all, I must get back… I find myself in Paris for an ugly business that's coming up. That's why I came all the way here in person."

He was on his feet. He looked at us with his jovial little eyes.

"An ugly business?" I stammered.

"A case of poisoning is always an ugly business."

Germaine in her turn murmured, "Poisoning!"

"That's what they suppose, anyway. Nothing has been proved yet. They still have to undertake an exhumation, carry out tests, make enquiries of pharmacists… a great deal of fuss, what? But I'm chattering on."

He made his way towards the door.

"See you soon, perhaps!"

Something inside me was vibrating like an over-taut violin string.

"Well now, Commissioner, a case of poisoning, you'll be in the news!"

"If it's proved, yes. So far we're still at the stage of gossip and anonymous denunciations."

"And… of course, the matter happened in your jurisdiction?"

"Of course!"

He hesitated. Finally he lowered his voice, as if frightened of being overheard.

"I'm all right telling you, it's about Crémant actually."

I already knew. Something more immediate than thought, stronger than intellect had warned me: instinct, basically.

"You know he was going through a divorce and you're acquainted with his wife? Those close to them think that... but, as I said, it remains to be proved."

His next gesture said "cop" loud and clear. Despite being bareheaded, he touched a finger to his temple.

"Goodbye, and apologies again. If the fellow in Nantes turns out to be Castain after all, phone me."

"Agreed."

He went away, leaving a man who had turned completely to jelly standing in the doorway.

At that moment I again felt the urge to reveal the truth to Germaine, and once more I refrained, still for the same reason.

The policeman's visit seemed untoward to me. I sensed I was on the brink of an abyss and that the slightest thing might send me over.

"You seem concerned," Germaine observed. "Do you think the man in Nantes...?"

"I don't know."

She stood up on the divan and wound her beautiful arms round my neck.

"What does it matter, darling? Even if it were Castain, you know I've made the leap now—I'll never go back to living with him."

She shook her head.

"I wonder what the commissioner must have thought when he saw we were together?"

I was wondering too; even so, I dispelled my companion's fears.

"He's thinking that you're a young woman, I'm a young man and Castain was a sick old rat… with those three factors, the outcome is obvious."

I left her and went to wash. The visit had demolished my joyful mood. A cold shower cleared my head to some extent. Still dripping, I stood in front of the washbasin mirror, gazing for a long time at my face, the face of a killer.

Looking myself up and down with a mean expression, I addressed myself in a low voice:

"You're in quite a mess here, Blaise my boy. It's one of two things, after all. Either that policeman has invented the whole poisoning thing because he suspects the truth and wants to see how you react, or else they seriously suspect the Crémant woman of having poisoned her husband, and in that case an exhumation is inevitable."

Either way I was losing.

"Are you speaking to me?" Germaine called from the studio.

"No."

"I thought…"

I was weary, although I hadn't been up for long. I felt as if I was on provisional release. All around me the walls were closing in. They were going to stifle me!

If I'd at least been able to examine the situation calmly! But no: I had to cheat, put on an act for Germaine. To start with, we had to go to Nantes to look at a man who could in no event be Castain.

Driven by the need to confess, I ran into the neighbouring room.

"Germaine!"

She was naked and doing gymnastic exercises to keep trim. It was a truly sensational sight.

"Yes, darling?"

I went up to her and put my arm round her supple waist.

"No, it's nothing!"

11

We were arriving at the Gare Montparnasse. As we reached the grand concourse I froze, feeling an urgent impulse to leave. But not to leave for Nantes…

"Listen, Germaine. You'll have to go alone."

She didn't immediately understand.

"The very idea!"

"Look, you can't go and identify a man suspected of being your husband in the company of your lover, it's a matter of simple respect."

"Fine, I'll go to the hospital on my own, but that doesn't stop you coming with me to Nantes!"

"It's too much for me, darling, I swear… I'm so afraid that it's him!"

"It's not him!"

She appeared sure of herself.

"You never know…"

She went on arguing for a long time, but I'd made my decision and in the end she listened to reason. I saw her settled on the train. We agreed to meet at the apartment the next day whatever happened, and then I left her, without waiting for the train to depart.

Three hours later I fetched up at my old Hôtel de la Gare. I needed to know where I stood, and for that I would have to find out whether the commissioner had been telling the truth.

Were there really rumours about the alleged poisoning of the property dealer? If not, then I had to beware, as that proved that the police had their eye on me. If there were, I had to make every effort to ensure that exhuming Crémant didn't prove fatal to me.

I had come by road, at the wheel of my hired Renault 4CV, concocting several plans to save my skin along the way. I valued my happiness, attained at such a high price, and was ready to do anything to safeguard it.

Arriving in the town which had been the scene of the most crucial event in my life, I felt myself overwhelmed by a kind of old sorrow. I found the place was smaller, greyer, more disquieting.

I stopped the car near the transformer next to the hotel and took a seat on the terrace.

The maid greeted me kindly.

"Well, M'sieur Delange, with us again?"

"For a few hours—I have some business to finish up."

Once informed, the owner was all over me:

"What a lovely surprise! This round's on me, M'sieur Delange."

"No thanks. We'll drink my health later."

He was bubbling over with curiosity.

"Nothing new on the… the matter?"

"Nothing!"

"Do you have news of Madame Castain?"

His pretence of innocence was so unconvincing he couldn't look at me.

I tapped him on the arm.

"Don't be a hypocrite—you know perfectly well we're living together, she and I."

"That's what people are saying…"

"'People' say a lot, say too much."

"My view exactly. Are you happy?"

"Very. A woman of twenty-eight and a man of fifty-two doesn't make for a happy marriage."

"Of course not."

"We liked each other, we proved it to each other, full stop, that's all."

Obsequiously, he agreed.

"And you were quite right."

"However," I went on, "we did not murder Castain, nor dispose of his body in quicklime."

He blushed.

"No one's saying that!"

"But everyone's thinking it…"

"Pfff, people, you know…"

"I know."

"They've got another hobby horse now."

We were getting there. I took a deep breath. Though it hardly improved my situation, deep down I would prefer it if the commissioner hadn't lied to me.

"Another hobby horse?"

"Yes. Concerning Crémant, you know, the property dealer."

"Yes?"

"They're saying he died very quickly and in a suspicious fashion… wagging tongues have it that his wife had a hand in it."

"Imagine that: poison?"

"Yes."

"And what does his doctor say?"

"Oh, that's Dr Boileau, he's very old, almost gaga… naturally he's stated that it's all nonsense and Crémant succumbed to peritonitis. We'll have to wait."

"What about the cops?"

"I think the commissioner is in quite a fix. He went to Paris to consult his superiors. It's clear that if the rumours are confirmed, they'll carry out a post-mortem on the body. The thing that makes it seem likely is the statement of the Crémants' maid, who claims that her mistress sent her to buy Colorado beetle powder shortly before the husband died. Colorado beetle powder! I ask you—their garden's all gravel. What use would that have been?"

I knew now what I'd wanted to know. I congratulated myself on coming here. I was in a position to influence the course of events. Just one thing, though: how?

Several hours of intense reflection led me to conclude I had only one way of ensuring my safety. For that, I absolutely had to take Castain's body out of the coffin it was in and get rid of it by some other means. What a strange task! At first sight, it appeared almost impossible. I no longer had authority to work in the cemetery, and even if I had still been employed by the funeral director's I would have been asked why I was reopening Crémant's vault just when the police were planning to do so. Yes, it was jolly delicate…

I took the car and headed towards the cemetery. Like all

places of its kind, it was outside the town. It was bounded to the front by the main road, on two sides by rough land which would one day be its annexe and lastly, on the fourth side, by the wall of a factory making chemical products.

There was no caretaker living nearby, which was a piece of luck. The nearest house was 200 metres away, on the main road.

What I was cooking up was terribly risky, but I had no choice. If I didn't remove Castain's corpse, the exhumation would prove I was guilty since no one but me could have put him in such a place.

To think that the local area saw more than a hundred deaths per year, all of them entirely natural, and I'd had to land on the single one that was suspicious!

Wasn't it a sign of Fate? Murder had attracted murder…

I returned to the town. In a suburban ironmonger's I bought a chisel, a large-headed hammer and a big screwdriver.

Next, I went back to the Hôtel de la Gare. I ate a substantial meal and said goodbye to the owner, assuring him I was hitting the road back to Paris. In reality I holed up in a quiet spot in the countryside to wait for nightfall.

I had grown used to the dead during my training with Castain, but my heart was beating faster than usual when, at nine in the evening, I scaled the cemetery gate.

By luck, if I may put it like that, the Crémant vault was at the other end of the cemetery, that is to say far from the road, near to the rough land. I found it quickly.

It stood out white against the darkness. Strong nerves were needed to withstand the terrifying atmosphere, and especially to get down to the task I'd decided to undertake.

The silence was disturbed only by the occasional calls of night birds, or by car horns sounding in the distance. The damp air stuck to your bronchial tubes... it tasted rather like soot. The cemetery exuded a nasty smell of rotting vegetation and damp earth. That smell was already the smell of death.

I got a grip on myself. This was not the moment to give in to fear. I dared not think the word, yet it kept coming into my head, sharp, icy. Fear! That bastard fear, which turns your legs weak, paralyses your throat and makes your chest burn.

I knelt down in front of the slab I was going to unseal. Taking the chisel, I wound its upper end in my silk scarf to deaden the blows of the hammer on its flat head.

I had never done this kind of work before, so I was infinitely clumsy at it. Often I brought the hammer down wide of the tool and it echoed eerily on the tomb slab.

Every little while, I stopped hammering in order to listen out, but each time I felt the night's chill silence, like a damp cloth, on my face.

Sweat streamed down my forehead and my back and fragments of cement peppered me in the face. At the outset I had crushed my left index finger and the wound was sending sharp pains all up my forearm. I managed to unseal the upper part of the stone, after a fashion. That left only the sides. I stood up for a moment as crouching down was making me go numb.

Silence still surrounded me. It should have been reassuring but instead it made me uneasy.

"What if the commissioner has laid a trap for you?" I thought.

What would happen if suddenly the sound of a whistle were to tear the silence and shadows climb over the perimeter walls?

I'd be caught. They'd put me in prison. Force me to confess. I'd be up in court. And then…

I took a deep breath to unblock my ears. I had antennae. I was picking up the indistinct rustlings which had to be caused by insects, or rodents. I was in a field of death. All around me, corpses had been planted.

"Blaise," I told myself, "you're a man. You have to go through with this. To the very end!"

So I picked up the chisel, the hammer… my scarf was in shreds. Try as I might to wrap it, the iron of the hammer rang out on the iron of the chisel.

It took me almost an hour to free the sides of the slab. It took me another to succeed in getting the cement cube off the top of the vault.

A burst of fetid air, stale and sickly sweet, overwhelmed me.

The most difficult part of the operation still remained to be done.

I let myself slip through the opening. The vault was deep. I felt around for a foothold with my toe. I thought I'd found one, but it was only the handle of a casket. It gave way under my weight and I fell to the bottom of the vault. A lightning-sharp pain tore through my ankle. Good God, I'd sprained it.

I groaned… I wanted to call for help. Never mind what happened next! Never mind everything! I was too scared. I was in too much pain. I looked up at the rectangle of clear sky above me.

There was water at the bottom of the vault. It had to be seeping in, surely.

I tried to stand up, but at the first attempt it proved impossible.

The horror of the situation was such that, paradoxically, I drew new courage from it. By gripping one of the cement shelves supporting a coffin, I managed to stand upright. I was wet and now my teeth were chattering… I moved, the pain in my leg grew unbearable. With every new action, my pain increased.

I had to hold out, no matter the cost. I couldn't allow myself to weaken.

The coffin containing the remains of the two "victims" was on a level with my chest. That made my job more complicated. Courageously, however, I set to. I had to feel my way, as the electric lamp I'd equipped myself with had been crushed in my pocket. Fortunately, the screws in the coffin protruded, making them easy to locate. I removed them one by one, being careful to slip them into my pocket so as not to lose them. I raised the lid; the smell which came from the casket was atrocious. But now I plunged into the horror with a kind of mild thrill.

I kept telling myself, "See it through, Blaise, see it through! You're paying for your crime right now. Everything has a price; this is your penance."

My hands rummaged around in the hideous box. They moved aside the shroud. I touched something hard and cold. Bracing myself against the wall of the tomb, I made sure of my hold and lifted it up. The corpse toppled over, taking me with it. We fell on top of each other in the muddy water covering the floor of the lair. The stinking mass was crushing me. There could be no greater horror than this. Even now, I wonder how my reason was able to overcome such a shock.

I pushed it over onto its side. There was the sound of a splash. I stood up, replaced the lid, put the screws back in position and took the screwdriver to them. Of course, it slipped out of my hands several times and I was forced to feel around in the water to recover it. At last, that side of things was finished.

I wiped my wet hands on my dry shirt front and searched my pockets for my box of matches. I wasn't that keen on seeing the place I was in but I was afraid of having dropped some personal item in the grave.

I rubbed one of the matchsticks against the rough part of the box. The little sulphurous gleam showed me a vision out of Dante. The coffins placed one on top of the other, the dead body lying on its side in the water, it all made me feel dizzy... Lighting three matches one after the other, I looked around the place: no, I hadn't lost anything and I was sure I wasn't leaving behind any personal item or telltale sign.

The pain in my ankle was calming down a little. I took hold of Castain by the upper torso. He was light, thankfully, and I had no great difficulty in getting him out of the grave. The hardest thing was extricating myself, because of my ankle, which seemed to explode as soon as I put any weight on it.

I managed, however, and then the damp, sweetish air in the cemetery seemed delightful compared to the stench of the pit.

I pivoted the stone to block off the opening again, then sealed it all round as best I could. Naturally it was a make-shift job and not worth the cement, but I didn't much care if people noticed the tomb had been broken into. The police would think it was connected to that other business.

Now that everything was finished in the cemetery, I was quivering with impatience. Oh to get this corpse far away from here, throw it into a hole, no matter where! What difference did it make? I had an alibi for the day of Castain's disappearance; the investigators would be very crafty indeed if they managed to prove my guilt.

I picked up my tools, slid them into my belt and, over-coming my repugnance, took hold of Castain by the waist. I held him pressed close and kept my head up, taking as few breaths as possible. I limped along, stifling a cry of pain at each step, knocking against gravestones, slipping in the soft mud of the cemetery.

The dead man weighed barely fifty kilos, and yet I had unbelievable trouble transporting him.

Once at the far side of the cemetery, I performed the whole exercise all over again. I leant him against the wall and hoisted him up by the ankles… he fell down on the other side of the wall before I'd had time to block my ears.

The dull thud he made as he hit the ground sent shockwaves right through me.

I scaled the wall in my turn. I knew my ankle must be very swollen and would keep me out of action for several days, but that wouldn't matter, once I'd succeeded in my undertaking.

I'd parked the 4CV in the shelter of the wall. Stowing a body in the little car constituted a new tour de force…

I slid in behind the wheel; luckily it was my left leg which was injured, because if it had been the right I wouldn't have been able to drive.

12

I must admit that at the wheel of my car, with this strange companion by my side, I was proud of myself. What I had accomplished was an exploit that very few men were capable of carrying out.

I covered several tens of kilometres, breathing the cool air coming in through the lowered window. The road stretched out, pale in the light from my headlamps. I met few vehicles and drove slowly, anxious to avoid an accident.

I went through several villages. After which, I stopped. I had to get rid of the dead man. My watch showed two o'clock, it would soon be dawn and I had to be back in Paris before daylight in order to tidy myself up. I was dirty, soaking wet, muddy, bleeding…

What should I do?

I looked around, peering into the darkness in search of an idea.

What could I do with this already decomposing corpse?

Then I had an idea—a new one, as good as the first from my point of view. Driving away again, I turned off the main road down a little byway to the left. I didn't know where this narrow, heavily rutted track led but my sense of direction told me it would join the Paris railway line.

And, indeed, after about four kilometres I spotted a railway embankment. A metal bridge went over the track. I pulled over onto the verge and examined the lie of the land. The track crossed an expanse of marshland, which was why it had been raised, despite being on a plain. At the foot of the embankment grew water plants, mainly reeds and rushes.

I pulled Castain from the car and, hoisting him onto my back, set off into the marshes, following the embankment. Struggling all the way, I covered a few hundred metres; I could go no farther as the ground was becoming less and less firm. I was sinking in halfway up my calves. Walking through mud is an arduous sport at the best of times, but when practised with a sprained ankle and a fifty-kilo load on your back, it borders on an epic feat!

I threw the corpse down at the foot of the embankment, lifting the legs up a little to make it look as though it had fallen from the railway track. Then, relieved, I finally went back to the car.

This series of exertions had wiped me out; I returned to the main road and allowed myself a few minutes' rest.

At five in the morning I stopped the car outside our flat. The door to the building was automatic, luckily, and there was no need to wake up the concierge in order to go in.

There was a broad mauve glow across the horizon. I groaned my way up the five storeys—there was no lift—went into the flat and leapt straight into the bathroom.

What a joy it was to be able to undress and sink into the hot water! My ankle had swollen to twice its normal size. It continued to be very painful; once in the bath, however, the pain lessened a little. I soaped myself like never before— I would have liked to be able to tear my skin off. Next I drenched myself in eau de cologne… it was terrific to feel safe… I had won. No one would ever know that, before being discovered at the foot of the embankment, Castain had spent a month in the coffin of one of his clients.

I buried my dirty linen in the laundry bag and put my suit on a coat hanger. It was a sorry sight. It was covered in mud, badly torn. I hung it near to the central-heating radiator to dry off.

After that I took a bottle of rum and limped over to the bed. I fell asleep after downing almost half a litre of the stuff…

I was woken by the sound of a bell. I looked at the little onyx clock in the studio. It showed eleven o'clock. The room was filled with sunshine. My head was ringing like a church tower on Easter morning. I felt dizzy… As the bell sounded again, I put on my dressing gown and went to open the door.

It was Germaine. Her face was grey from the train. Her features looked drawn.

"You're still in bed!" she exclaimed in astonishment.

"Yes, imagine—on my way back from the station yesterday I tripped and twisted my ankle."

I showed her my swollen leg; the injured ankle was even thicker now than in the early hours and was turning a nasty purple colour. Germaine was alarmed.

"I'll get a doctor, you need to have that strapped up!"

I realized just then that I was forgetting to ask her the outcome of her visit to the hospital in Nantes.

"Well then?"

"What do *you* think? The guy they showed me is fifteen years younger than Achille!"

She helped me over to the bed and went to tell the concierge to call a doctor.

When she came back up I held out my arms: "We haven't kissed yet, Germaine!"

"True... and it's not that I don't want to. How long that trip seemed..."

As I'd suspected, I had given myself a sprain. I had to stay in bed for a week before I was able to move about, with my ankle seriously bandaged. But that week of being cooped up seemed short to me. I truly savoured it. Germaine was an adorable nurse, so gentle and attentive. In her company the time passed almost without my being aware of it.

We made many plans for the future. We were resolved to leave Paris and take a small shop in a town on the Côte d'Azur. Germaine wanted a bookshop, because she loved reading and selling books seemed somehow noble to her; I shared her tastes. I could already see myself ensconced in a smart new shop, surrounded by volumes in many different colours... Only, for us to have that, poor Castain's body had to be found and his death duly certified.

I was in a hurry for us to pass that ultimate test. After that, we truly would be free.

It wasn't long before my wish was granted. The following week, we received a police summons inviting us both to present ourselves at the gendarmerie in Nofflet "for a matter concerning us".

The piece of paper made Germaine blanch.

To me it was perfectly clear, because I remembered seeing a signpost with the name of that town on the road to the embankment.

"Do you think he's been found?"

"It's possible."

"What should we do?"

"That's a good one—go, of course!"

And so we went.

13

On Germaine's return from Nantes, I had got her to telephone the garage which had rented us the car to tell them to come and pick it up from outside my building. There was no point in keeping it since I couldn't drive. Besides, after what I'd used it for, I wasn't keen on hanging on to it.

To go to Nofflet I rented another car. This time I chose a Peugeot 203, because it was very possible that some poacher had noticed the 4CV on the night of the… transfer. We had to take precautions on every side; innocent details often prove the undoing of the most skilfully contrived intrigues.

At three in the afternoon we rang at the gate of a country house surmounted by a handsome new tricolour.

A bareheaded gendarme called to us to come in from his office doorway. We set off up a stony path strewn with toys. The gendarme observed us suspiciously. He was a tall devil with a receding hairline, a broad nose with a turned-up tip and round, beady eyes which made me think of a duck's.

"What's this about?"

I held out the summons. He nodded his head and his manner softened.

"Ah yes, I see."

He came out of the room and looked up the stairwell, calling "Boss!"

After which he came back in and offered us two chairs sticky with dirt.

"We would like to know…" I began.

He interrupted me with a gesture. He threw a meaningful look in Germaine's direction and, to give himself something to do while we waited for his superior's arrival, began to roll himself a cigarette using a little gadget fixed to his tobacco pouch.

The senior officer was young with a thin, honest face.

"Madame, monsieur…"

He had put his peaked cap very straight on his head, which made him look like a character on an old recruitment poster.

"You are Madame Castain?"

Germaine gave a brief nod. She was tense, concentrating. The officer was looking at her fondly. He found her so attractive that he didn't think of hiding his admiration.

"Have you found him?" I asked.

"Yes."

"Is he… dead?"

He was watching Germaine closely, no doubt fearing she might pass out. But Germaine remained motionless on her chair, chin up, gazing uncertainly at him.

"Where?" I went on.

"In some marshland alongside the railway. He must have fallen from the train and his body was half-hidden by the rushes."

There, it was over at last. None of us knew what to say. I think the cops were more embarrassed than we were.

"When was he found?" Germaine asked.

"Yesterday morning. It was a railwayman inspecting the track who noticed him. We notified your local police station as soon as his identity had been established. The station gave us your address and asked us to summon you right away, as well as monsieur…"

He was struck by a sudden thought: "Are you a relative?"

I blushed.

"Not exactly… I was Monsieur Castain's employee."

Instantly he grew suspicious, realizing that the situation Germaine and I were in was rather irregular.

"Might he have been pushed from the train?" enquired Germaine, as if in reply to a hidden thought on the officer's part.

The latter gave a shrug.

"That will be for the investigating officers to establish. He wasn't robbed, at any rate. I found his papers and his money on him… nearly twenty thousand francs! And his watch."

"Any signs of injury?" I asked.

"No, except a small bruise on the chin, resulting from his fall, no doubt. I'm going to ask you to be so kind as to identify the body."

Germaine appeared to wake up. The colour had drained from her lips.

"I…"

"Do you feel that's too much for you, madame?"

She hesitated.

"No."

"Then if you'd like to follow me…"

*

Castain's corpse had been left on the cart used to carry him here. The sinister vehicle had been stored in a shed adjacent to the town hall. A worn tarpaulin was covering Achille's remains; the gendarmerie officer slid it off. He watched us as he removed the cloth. Germaine dared not look. She seemed wary. Finally, she risked a furtive glance towards the black mass that was her husband. I was standing by her side, ready to hold her.

"It's horrendous," she sighed.

In the bright light of day, Castain's body no longer frightened me.

He was as pitiful as all the clients to whose homes I had accompanied him. He was a very banal dead man... a mud-stained, stinking dead man who inspired more disgust than pity. In his lifetime Castain had looked like a nonentity, and he was no more majestic in death.

"Come on," I murmured, taking hold of Germaine by the arm. "What's the point of looking at that?"

"'That' is a dead man," grumbled the officer, replacing the tarpaulin.

As we stepped out of the shed, a black Citroën Traction Avant full of men drew up in front of the town hall with a great screeching of brakes. Among the newcomers I recognized the commissioner who had visited us in Paris. He was escorted by two other figures and the gendarme from before. He came over to us looking concerned.

"May I offer you my condolences, Madame Castain?"

"Thank you."

After which he made the introductions.

"Chief Inspector Charvieux and his colleague Houdet…"

The chief had an unpleasant face, covered in freckles, steel-grey eyes and the most pronounced dimple I've ever seen on a chin.

Our police commissioner must have told him about us, because he spoke to me as if we'd known each other for aeons.

"What have you got to say about this?" he asked me point-blank.

"What do you expect me to say about it? In one sense it's a relief."

"For whom?"

"For Madame Castain in the first instance, and then for me. It's depressing to have a missing person hanging over your head."

He took my arm, casually, the way Italians do in the evening to have a talk.

"Tell me, you're living with the little lady, it appears?"

"Yes. Why? Are you shocked?"

"Not me, I've seen it all. But it proves to me that you have… umm… feelings for each other. Now since I'm a cop I'm wondering whether those feelings didn't manifest themselves before! Do you follow me?"

I kept my cool incredibly well.

"Perfectly. In short, you're saying to yourself that, since we love each other, we must have got rid of Castain, yes?"

"In short, yes. We have twisted minds in the police, you know!"

He remained calm, but his grey eyes were making me uneasy.

"You haven't answered my question. Were you Germaine Castain's lover before her spouse disappeared?"

"To some extent, but the thought of throwing him in front of a moving train would never have entered my head, nonetheless."

"No?"

"No."

"And yet a cuckolded husband is an inconvenience."

"Not him."

"Why not?"

"Because while he was there we had no desire to live together, Germaine and I."

"But love gives rise to that desire."

"You don't know Germaine. She's the kind of little woman who has scruples."

"Those have their limits, though, don't they?"

"If her flesh is weak, her character is less so. Castain had to disappear before she would agree to follow me. Let's say I took advantage of the fact that she was upset."

Suddenly he left me standing there and, without a word to Germaine, went into the shed. The police commissioner had gone in ahead of him. He came back out and made for us.

"Well, there you are," he sighed. "The dead never stay hidden for long, you see…"

Germaine seemed overcome after seeing her husband's body.

"That's one of your mysteries solved, Commissioner."

He frowned.

"One of my mysteries?"

"Good God, I'm thinking of the business with the poisoning that you spoke to us about."

He shrugged.

"Oh, that matter's been sorted for three days now."

I thought I would collapse in a heap at his feet.

"Has it?"

"Yes. Comparing the Crémants' maid's testimony with that of the chemist where she claimed to have bought the Colorado beetle powder put an end to it. In reality it was DDT that Madame Crémant had ordered. Moreover, the doctor said again he was certain the death was due to natural causes."

"And… you haven't exhumed the body?"

"Do you think that can be done just like that? If we had to listen to gossip we'd spend all our time getting the grave-diggers out!"

I could have cried. I had taken enormous risks, I'd shivered with fright for a whole night, I'd gone down into a grave to lug corpses about, I'd sprained my ankle, I'd… Well, at least Germaine was genuinely a widow now. We were going to get our hands on old Castain's dosh and someday soon get married. All things considered, I hadn't wasted my time…

Chief Inspector Charvieux reappeared, hat pushed to the back of his head.

All three of us looked at him enquiringly.

"Very odd," he said. "He didn't have a train ticket on him… yet if the picture people have given me is to be believed, he wasn't the sort of man to travel without paying his fare."

"Perhaps he lost it when he fell?" I suggested.

"We'll be going over the site of the accident with a fine-toothed comb. It's also strange that no one saw him at the station… And wasn't he supposed to be going to Paris along with a friend?"

"That's what he told me."

The commissioner took over.

"This friend, did he talk about him before or after we'd met at the Crémants' home?"

"After!"

"When?"

I thought about what my reply should be. I was on slippery ground.

"We went to place the body in the church. While I was preparing the catafalque, Castain went out to fetch the big black drapery from the hearse. He was away for a little while… then he told me he'd just met a friend who was going to drive him to Paris."

"And then?" Charvieux persisted.

"Then nothing. He shook my hand and left."

"And you?"

"What about me?"

"What did you do then?"

"I arranged the flowers, after which I went back to the shop. Madame Castain will tell you that."

"And that afternoon?"

"I did the accounts at the house."

"And you didn't leave the town?"

"Not until I went to Paris, ten days later."

He made a sign to his colleague, who was taking notes with the gendarmes.

"Take down the address of the lady and gentleman."

The other, a mean, grubby-looking little man, wrote down the information as I dictated it.

Once this formality had been completed, I asked, "And now what happens?"

Charvieux shrugged his shoulders: "Nothing special... plan the funeral... it can take place immediately after the post-mortem."

That word had me worried, but I kept my composure. After all, a post-mortem couldn't reveal anything positive. I had killed Castain by suffocating him under a thick layer of cloth. Now, death by suffocation *is a natural death. Or rather, a natural death is the inevitable result of suffocation.*

I had nothing to fear. *Nothing!*

The cops wouldn't be able to make head nor tail of it. What would save me was the fact that the whole thing had happened at two different times. Firstly, murder followed by complete disappearance of the body. Next, discovery of the body far away from the town, but a watertight alibi for me the whole time it was missing...

These gentlemen would be forced to conclude it was an accident, with or without a train ticket. They weren't about to saddle themselves with an insoluble case just for want of a little rectangular piece of cardboard. For once they had the opportunity to close the case file nice and quietly.

More and more I regretted inventing the detail of the obliging friend! That was the cracked bell which sounded a false note in their ears.

But what did it matter? Perhaps it would cover the tracks.

I offered Germaine my arm.

"Come on."

We were at a loss, and could feel the crushing weight of the cops' stares on the back of our heads.

14

At the time of Castain's disappearance, the newspapers had reported the fact—the regional ones mainly—but rather discreetly, as if holding back. They were wary. This might be a simple case of someone running away. Afterwards their readers would have been angry with them if they'd made a big thing of it.

Two days after the body was discovered, they made up for it. The press struck up a chorus of "The Railway Corpse". Now *there* was a title for a pre-war detective novel... All the journalists focused on the fact that the dead man had no ticket on him, but had not been robbed. They also mentioned that the police had ordered a post-mortem, the results of which would be forthcoming—somewhat alarming, but I was reassured by the evening papers. One of them had interviewed the forensic pathologist. The man of science hadn't yet begun his unpleasant task, but let it be known that *a priori* the corpse showed no suspicious signs...

Reading this led me to understand that we had the advantage. I became downright optimistic two days later, when I read a statement by an employee at the Gare d'Austerlitz who claimed to have seen Castain running for his train on the day he disappeared.

I don't know where the guy had got that from! At all events, he was positive: he recognized "The Railway Corpse"—a photo of whom had been printed in the papers—perfectly.

No doubt he was confusing him with another passenger. Or, more simply, he was keen to make himself interesting. The world is full of obscure people who try to emerge from the shadows via the narrow path of the minor news stories.

If you accepted this statement as true, you could, according to the press, make the following argument: Castain genuinely *had* come to Paris with a driver friend, and once in the capital he had abandoned the idea of visiting his doctor for some reason. That evening he had meant to return home by train but, arriving at the station at the last minute, had not had time to buy a ticket. Indeed, he had run after the train which was moving off, no doubt intending to pay his fare to a ticket collector. A good part of the journey had passed off without incident, before Castain, who had a reputation for being tight-fisted, had said to himself it would be stupid not to travel the whole way without paying. He had perched on the step of the carriage to evade the ticket collector, lost his balance and fallen to his death.

Besides the all-important statement from the station worker, what confirmed this hypothesis was the fact that the body was lying on the same side of the tracks as the trains coming *down* from Paris. He had therefore fallen on his way back from Paris, not on the way there.

I was well and truly saved.

Since she had come face-to-face with the dead man, all the life had gone out of Germaine. She no longer left our studio and it was I who went shopping. She spent her days curled up on the divan in her see-through negligee. She would push

137

me away firmly whenever I tried to take her in my arms. She spoke rarely, and in such a wretched tone that it pained me to hear her.

I made no attempt to combat the dejection resulting from the shock she had experienced. I thought that once Castain was buried for good, events would resume their course. The future was ours; besides, I understood her attitude. She was prey to remorse. Now that Achille's death was established, she could recognize her fickleness. She was ashamed at having left the marital home so quickly to follow her lover. The town's populace must think her a vile little tart, and she had too great a sense of personal respectability not to suffer cruelly from this collective disapproval.

The evening following our visit to Nofflet she had written to her lawyer instructing him to arrange the funeral and the liquidation of assets.

"I'm never going back there!" she informed me.

"But what about the funeral?"

"They can bury him without me."

I knew she was stubborn so I did not insist. After all, she was right. There was no need to go along with the proprieties. Since I had to wait, I would wait.

By the third day there was no longer any mention of Castain in the newspapers. I breathed easy: this time the matter was finished with. I felt light, happy.

I was determined to lift Germaine's spirits.

"If you'd like," I said to her, "we can leave for the Côte d'Azur next week. We'll look for the bookshop of our dreams."

"Yes, Blaise."

She didn't know the South of France. I described it in rhapsodic terms. But no matter how much I praised the palm trees, the mimosa, the blue sea and the sun, she was unable to throw off her languor.

I began to be seriously worried. Surely she wasn't going to start missing Castain! That wretch who had given her more beatings than embraces!

When I could bear it no longer, I raised the subject.

"Germaine, can you explain to me what's going on inside you?"

She looked up at me with pale eyes filled with astonishment.

"What's going on inside me?"

"Don't play the innocent. Since… the other day it's as if you're no longer with me! Are you sad?"

She shook her head.

"Oh no."

"Do you feel guilty?"

Incredibly, she appeared not to understand my question.

"Guilty. Why would I?"

"I don't know… for having come here, now you know he was dead."

She shrugged.

"No, Blaise, I made my choice a long time ago."

"What then?"

Her face was grave. She was like the first image I'd had of her in the post office.

She gave me that same preoccupied, absent look.

"It's something else, Blaise."

"Something else? But what, darling?"

"I'd like to ask you a question."

"I'm listening."

"Swear to me that you'll answer truthfully."

I felt myself shivering inside. I was cold, like in the Crémant vault the other night.

"This is all very formal. Look here, Germaine…"

"Swear!"

My voice hoarse, I stuttered "I swear to you."

She drew into herself, looking for the exact words to express what she was thinking.

"Blaise, where had you put him for all that time?"

I shut my eyes. For three seconds, everything in me stopped. I became empty, felt nothing.

"What are you saying?!"

Without meaning to, I had shouted… a poor shield to cover my panic.

"Listen, Blaise. When they showed me Achille's body, do you know the first thing I noticed? His clothes were covered in a layer of red mud, *like yours were when I came back from Nantes!*"

There was nothing I could say. Her perceptiveness terrified me.

"All at once," she sighed, "I knew that you had killed Achille. I don't know how or when. I've been thinking about it for three days now and I still don't understand. What puzzles me the most is the hiding place… because you hid his body until the other night, didn't you?"

For the first time I resisted temptation, the temptation to confess to her.

"You're mad, Germaine! Completely mad! Your story about the mud is absurd."

She tossed her blonde hair.

"And you swore to answer me…"

"I am answering you, Germaine, and my answer is 'no'. Your imagination's playing tricks on you."

"You swore to answer me truthfully!"

"Oh good God in heaven, I'm telling you…"

She made a weary gesture.

"Fine, don't shout. I must be mistaken."

"You are mistaken!"

She had dropped her head. I made her raise it again by lifting up her chin.

"You have to believe me, Germaine. If you don't believe me our love will be lost!"

"I believe you…"

Stupidly, it was my turn to say:

"Swear it!"

She hesitated. I was about to get angry when the doorbell rang.

15

The concierge didn't keep pressing on the bell like that, nor the delivery men. Germaine went to open the door. I heard her greet someone, then she showed Charvieux and his inspector into the studio. The chief had a stye in his eye which detracted from his authority.

He was holding his felt hat between two fingers and wearing a Gestapo-style green raincoat.

He had turned up at a moment when I really could have done without him.

"Good day, Inspector, what chance brings you here?"

He smiled at me.

"When we go to someone's house, you know, it's rarely by chance…"

There was a pile of newspapers on the floor. He pointed to them.

"It seems to be blowing over, eh?"

"I should be asking *you* that."

Charvieux bowed his head slightly but his eyes never left me. Despite the prominent stye he was no longer at all ridiculous.

"Oh, if you ask my opinion, I'll tell you it's getting more complicated."

My eyes sought Germaine. She had just sat down on the divan. Legs crossed, hands folded on top of them, she was listening attentively.

"It's getting more complicated?" I echoed.

"I'd say so…"

I wouldn't wish anyone to go through a silence like the one which set in then. It made you want to scream with impatience.

"Well then, spit it out," I growled. "What are you playing at? Frightening us?"

Charvieux reacted like a true cop: he slapped me.

Germaine cried out, stood up, then sat down again. My cheek was burning. I told myself that if there was ever a moment to keep my dignity, this was it. Charvieux seemed not in the least put out by his angry gesture.

"I'm playing at finding out what you were playing at with Castain," he said.

The other policeman chuckled. He thought that was brilliant, and it seemed to make him respect his superior even more.

"Castain? What now?"

"You'll be told very soon. Put your things on, both of you."

"Are you arresting us?"

"That's not the right word, but…"

He gave a malicious smile.

"Something like that."

"Madame as well?"

"Madame Castain as well. Aren't you joined together for better and for worse?"

"Do you have a warrant?"

"No, but that's a simple formality the examining magistrate will agree to. I can send my inspector to fetch two if you insist… that'll give you an extra hour."

"At least tell me what for."

"As if you didn't know."

"But no, I…"

"Oh, that's enough—we'll talk about it in my office. I want to interview you separately."

I was about to protest again. It was Germaine who calmed me down.

"Look, Blaise, do as you're told."

We dressed in silence.

We were separated almost without noticing, by a trick with the doors. We were walking side by side, escorted by the two policemen. The chief's assistant pushed open a leather-padded door, and we stood aside to let Germaine go in. He followed her. The door shut once more. Then Charvieux touched my arm and led me farther on into another office.

"Sit down, Delange!"

I was more than a little unsure of myself. I understood now why suspects spill the beans so easily. Police protocol is disturbing. No sooner was I through the door than I was already thinking like a guilty man.

"Don't you have anything to tell me about Castain's death?"

"What do you want me to tell you?"

"Who poisoned him, for example."

I must have misheard.

"Who p—?"

"Yes, poisoned. The toxicologists' report is definite. Poisoning by a solution of arsenic salts. The pathologist thought he could see traces; they did some tests on the hair, and the amount of poison present in it leaves no room for doubt."

The policeman explained this to me kindly, the way he would have explained it to a friend.

"So, with poisoning established, it remains to ascertain who poured the poison into Castain's food, as that has to be how the poison was administered."

I made no reply. I didn't understand.

Castain, poisoned? That was stupid. I was the one who knew how he'd been killed. Poison! Come on…

"What do you say to that?"

He was taking his time, that bastard of a cop. He was so sure of himself. Poor idiot, going along with the experts, experts who saw poison everywhere.

"You used to have your midday meal at the Castains'?"

"Why are you asking me, since you already know?"

He must have been used to such rebuffs. It did not put him out.

"Do I look like someone who puts poison in a person's glass?"

"I know it's not a man's weapon. That's why I'm inclined to believe his wife is the guilty one and you're complicit."

"That's not true—Germaine's innocent!"

"It has to be one of you."

"If you knew Madame Castain, the idea that she could have done that wouldn't even cross your mind."

"That's just it, I'm trying to get to know her… I'll question her after my inspector. Women are harder to crack than men."

He got up and walked round his desk.

"She poisoned him! I can feel it!"

"No."

"Shut it, let me speak. Castain had a seizure and died... you concealed his body."

"I won't let you say that to me, your accusation is an insult. It's vile to behave like this."

"Oh, give up, old man. Other people have been outraged in this office, others who have got on their high horse like you, and who are nonetheless sewing slippers behind bars at Poissy!"

"We didn't poison Castain. I give you my..."

"Your word of honour? It remains to be seen what your honour is worth, Delange. I can feel I'm getting near the truth. Poison was the wife's idea, she administered it... the husband died and you hid the body to avoid a post-mortem."

"Seriously, do you actually believe what you're saying?"

"Well?"

"Fine, supposing I *had* hidden the body to avoid a post-mortem. Would I have hidden it right below the railway track so a railwayman would find it?"

"Not right away."

I gave a start. He seemed to know a lot about it, despite his fundamental mistake.

"What do you mean, not right away?"

"The corpse was brought there. The clothes were coated with completely different soil from that of the embankment."

I should have thought of that. If Germaine had noticed that detail, it wouldn't have escaped the police.

I had to protest. Silence would have been my downfall.

"So I'd found such a good hiding place that the police hadn't been capable of finding the missing man's body and then when they'd stopped searching I'd have been idiotic enough to take it out of there so that it would be discovered?"

"Yes."

"Well then, Inspector, the cat's got my tongue."

"Better get it back then—you'll need it to make your defence."

"I thought the police always proceeded by logic even when they were wrong?"

"I am proceeding by logic, Delange. It takes seven years before a missing person is presumed dead and their beneficiaries inherit."

"Is that all?"

"Yes. You weren't unaware of that. You didn't want to hang around for seven years before getting your hands on old Castain's money, eh? So you went to recover the dead man from his hiding place and you put him down beneath the railway track to make people think he'd come to grief falling from the train."

"Wonderful, you should write books."

"When I retire, perhaps."

"And yet I read a certain statement by a certain employee at Austerlitz…"

"A drunk! In order to board a train you need at least a platform ticket. How do you explain the fact that Castain had time to get one of those rather than his train ticket?"

"I don't have to explain anything. You're accusing me and I'm defending myself. I didn't poison Castain, and I wasn't an accomplice in his poisoning. Furthermore, he wasn't poisoned."

"And?"

"And nothing. Arrest me or let me go, I'm not saying any more. I deny it, full stop, end of story. Got that?"

By way of answer, he picked up the receiver. He did not dial a number, as it was an internal telephone. He simply told the switchboard operator:

"Get me Judge Solivot!"

There was a crackling on the line.

"Judge Solivot? Charvieux here. Would you issue me with two arrest warrants for the couple in the Castain case?"

The couple in the Castain case? I was more struck by that than by his request. So in these gentlemen's eyes we already had a label. I sensed all the calculation, all the finality of the designation.

"It's a miscarriage of justice," I said in a flat voice.

He seemed sincere when he blurted out, "Heaven forbid, Delange! I know you and she are guilty. I'm an old fox, I can't possibly be mistaken."

"And you're accusing us based on a gut feeling?"

"No, on presumptions and near-proofs."

He pressed a buzzer on his desk. Some guards came in. He pointed at me without uttering a word. The cops gestured to me to stand up.

I knew it was pointless to resist. They were stronger.

At that moment, for the first time in my adult life, I wanted to cry.

I thought with tenderness of the streets which continued, outside, being streets for people... the people who were free people.

16

There is nothing like the first night in prison to cause you to reflect on the precarious nature of life in general and of happiness in particular. Happiness: is that even possible?

I didn't sleep a wink all night. It wasn't finding myself in a cell which disheartened me the most, but that unforeseeable bolt from the blue: Castain's poisoning.

I had prepared my defence on a completely different basis and here I was, being asked hard questions on a topic I hadn't swotted up, for the excellent reason that I hadn't been aware of it.

Lying fully dressed on the narrow bed, I turned the problem over in my mind for hours. I knew full well that the police were mistaken. I hadn't poisoned Castain, and anyone who believed Germaine guilty really didn't know her. And yet there was poison in the corpse! There had to be an explanation for this phenomenon.

Had there been a mistake at the pharmacy where he bought his medicines? There had been similar cases. My imagination started to race. And then suddenly I'd got it. It was dazzling. *I knew who had poisoned Castain!* The guilty man's name was Crémant and *he had died before his victim!* The troubling rumours which had threatened the safety of the property dealer's widow were founded. The eccentric Romanian woman had indeed poisoned her husband, as people's whispers had it.

I had read accounts of cases like this. They had taught me that arsenic is a poison which spreads; corpses which had been disinterred carried it simply because the soil in the cemetery contained it.

The more deeply I thought about the matter, the surer I became that the arsenic found on Castain had come from the man he had shared the coffin with.

There was no doubt: it was Crémant who had been poisoned. Afterwards, when the two dead men had found themselves face to face, he had transmitted some of his arsenic to Castain.

When I examined the way events had unfolded, I discovered the monstrous machinations of chance. Ever since the post office where I had seen Germaine coming out of the telephone booth, I'd been trapped in its malign workings. For a long time it had seemed to me that I was in control of Fate, but in reality I was only its quiescent servant.

Suddenly I was afraid of justice... not of men's justice, no: that is on a human scale. But of another justice, more implacable, more infallible—more immanent!

"You're not going to get out of this," I told myself. "Charvieux has got you now and he'll see it through to the end because he has already gone too far to be able to stop. Armed with the old saying, 'Look for the one who benefits from the crime,' he'll be ruthless in pursuit of Germaine and me."

She was the one I was thinking of. The idea that at that very moment she was looking at the blue nightlight of a cell when she was innocent caused me pain. Poor love... she'd

151

had no luck with men. She had been conceived and put on this earth to be a peaceful spouse, and up to now she had only been the partner of an invalid, a maniac and a killer.

If I denied it, she would become the police's target. The chief had said it: poison is a woman's weapon… No, I wouldn't. Germaine had been let down too much, abused too much, deceived too much. She was entitled to peace, if not to happiness.

At ten o'clock the next morning, I was taken back into Charvieux's office. He had changed out of his suit and was now wearing a suede jacket with crumpled lapels and a canary-yellow shirt. His stye was a little better but continued to lend him a strange asymmetrical, swollen look.

"How're you, Delange?"

"Not good."

"Bad night?"

"Very bad."

"Have you thought about the questions I put to you yesterday?"

Why was he so sure of himself? He seemed not to have the slightest doubt as to the outcome of his inquiry. This devil knew his fellow men. He could tell the difference between those who were hiding something and the others.

I felt desolate and calm.

"I have thought about them, Chief Inspector."

"And?"

"Would you mind calling a clerk? All this is very long and complicated; I have no wish to tell it several times over."

A delighted sparkle came into his eyes. He called something from his office doorway, and a fat lump of an inspector came and sat down at the typewriter. A man with three chins, wearing on his little finger a gold signet ring as big as a papal ring.

"We're all ears, Delange."

I hesitated. I found myself on the brink of the abyss. It was still possible for me to get away.

I closed my eyes in order to concentrate. When you accept what I was about to accept, you have to be very sure of your decision.

Charvieux, hands folded on his desk, was silent. When I opened my eyes again, I saw he was looking out of the window at the trees in the Quai des Orfèvres.

He must have been thinking about the same things as I was, only from a different angle.

I cleared my throat and crossed my legs to make myself believe I was relaxed.

And then I took the plunge: "Well, Inspector..."

Afterwards my throat was dry from talking. The typewriter had fallen silent at the same time as I had. The fat cop was massaging his fingers and loosening his shoestring tie. Charvieux was pulling at the lapels of his suede jacket to smooth them down.

"Is that it?"

"Yes, Inspector. Don't you believe me?"

"Your version, with the poison spreading from the dead man, doesn't stand up."

"Eh?"

"I'm going to consult the experts and ask for Crémant to be exhumed."

He was no longer in the least cordial. It was cop and suspect now. He had me returned to my cell, where I spent several days with no news from anyone. Those hours I lived through in suspense weighed on me like so many years. I could not take in the fact that it was all over. Never again would I know freedom, nor a woman's love. They would try me… maybe even send me to the guillotine, although I didn't think so, because the motive behind all this was passion. Here in France juries are susceptible to love.

It would take time for me to understand that, in the blink of an eye, I had gone from peaceful happiness to the blackest despair. It would take me much longer still to accept it.

When eventually I went back into Charvieux's office, Germaine was there along with some more officers. I was struck by her jaundiced complexion and distracted look. I smiled at her.

"Hello, Germaine."

She moved her head slightly.

"Sit down," the chief told me.

My old suspect's chair, with its straw seat and bars that turned round under my feet when I leant on them to shift my position.

Charvieux had a pile of forbidding-looking papers in front of him.

"Delange, we have exhumed Crémant. Let me tell you right away, it's as I thought: your story doesn't stand up. He died of natural causes. Not the slightest trace of poison according to our experts here."

He brandished other pieces of paper.

"Contamination by the arsenic would have been impossible in such a short space of time. Besides, some was found in Castain's stomach."

He was not bluffing. Detailed, ratified, stamped reports proved it.

I looked at Germaine. Her face said it all. *She* was the poisoner! I recalled the undertaker's stomach troubles, his nausea, his waxen complexion, his weak spells. For weeks she had administered his death drop by drop. That was her way of fighting back against the blows and all the acts of pettiness.

Charvieux was looking at us.

"I've brought you together again with the firm resolve to find out the truth. The real truth. Do you hear me? Which of you put this filthy stuff into Castain's system? Eh? Come on, out with it, kids. It's time."

I got to my feet. I could stay still no longer. It was as if my legs had a life of their own.

"Oh, very well. It was me, Inspector, me alone. I wanted to get rid of him this way, and when I found out he was going to Paris for treatment, I was afraid the doctors would discover the truth. So I rushed things along, and took advantage of the opportunity that presented itself."

I didn't look at anyone. It's difficult to lie in those conditions.

155

Charvieux's voice rang out, suspicious:

"Why did you invent that story about arsenic spreading in the grave?"

"I hoped people would believe me. Because, after all, poisoning like that implies premeditation, doesn't it? And I think I can safely say that goes down very badly in court."

"And Madame Castain was your accomplice?"

I shrugged.

"Do you think it takes a whole gang to pour a pinch of powder into a glass?"

"Did she know what you were doing?"

"Absolutely not!"

"Madame Castain, you weren't aware of the poisoning attempt?"

"No."

"And… afterwards?"

"Again, no."

I looked at Germaine.

"If she had known, she wouldn't have stayed with me one minute longer, would you, darling?"

Her eyes were gentle as never before. I saw that she was accepting the sacrifice I was making. Not selfishly, because it got her out of a sticky situation, but as an homage I was paying to our love.

She sensed that, in saving her, I was saving something inside myself far more precious than my life or my freedom.

"No," she murmured. "I wouldn't have stayed with you, Blaise."

With another look, I thanked her for accepting my gift.

Then I slumped back into my chair, weary like a man who has just finished a hard day's work.

When I looked round again to try to see her once more, she was no longer there...

They had sent her out into life again, all on her own.

———

ALSO AVAILABLE FROM PUSHKIN VERTIGO

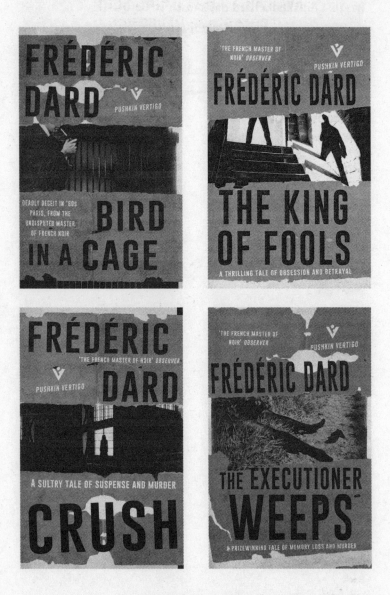

FRÉDÉRIC DARD

PUSHKIN VERTIGO

DEADLY DECEIT IN '60S PARIS, FROM THE UNDISPUTED MASTER OF FRENCH NOIR

BIRD IN A CAGE

'THE FRENCH MASTER OF NOIR' *OBSERVER*

PUSHKIN VERTIGO

FRÉDÉRIC DARD

THE KING OF FOOLS

A THRILLING TALE OF OBSESSION AND BETRAYAL

FRÉDÉRIC

'THE FRENCH MASTER OF NOIR' *OBSERVER*

PUSHKIN VERTIGO

DARD

A SULTRY TALE OF SUSPENSE AND MURDER

CRUSH

'THE FRENCH MASTER OF NOIR' *OBSERVER*

PUSHKIN VERTIGO

FRÉDÉRIC DARD

THE EXECUTIONER WEEPS

A PRIZEWINNING TALE OF MEMORY LOSS AND MURDER

Find out more at **www.pushkinpress.com**

AVAILABLE AND COMING SOON
FROM PUSHKIN VERTIGO

Jonathan Ames
You Were Never Really Here

Augusto De Angelis
The Murdered Banker
The Mystery of the Three Orchids
The Hotel of the Three Roses

Olivier Barde-Cabuçon
Casanova and the Faceless Woman

María Angélica Bosco
Death Going Down

Piero Chiara
The Disappearance of Signora Giulia

Frédéric Dard
Bird in a Cage
The Wicked Go to Hell
Crush
The Executioner Weeps
The King of Fools
The Gravediggers' Bread

Friedrich Dürrenmatt
The Pledge
The Execution of Justice
Suspicion
The Judge and His Hangman

Martin Holmén
Clinch
Down for the Count
Slugger

Alexander Lernet-Holenia
I Was Jack Mortimer

Margaret Millar
Vanish in an Instant

Boileau-Narcejac
Vertigo
She Who Was No More

Leo Perutz
Master of the Day of Judgment
Little Apple
St Peter's Snow

Soji Shimada
The Tokyo Zodiac Murders
Murder in the Crooked Mansion

Masako Togawa
The Master Key
The Lady Killer

Emma Viskic
Resurrection Bay
And Fire Came Down
Darkness for Light

Seishi Yokomizo
The Inugami Clan
Murder in the Honjin